To: Jim

Keeping the Promise

By

Alyce Godbey

Cora Alyce Godbey Seaman
4/07

1663 LIBERTY DRIVE, SUITE 200
BLOOMINGTON, INDIANA 47403
(800) 839-8640
WWW.AUTHORHOUSE.COM

This book is a work of fiction. People, places, events, and situations are the product of the author's imagination. Any resemblence to actual persons, living or dead, or historical events, is purely coincidental.

© 2005 Alyce Godbey. All Rights Reserved.

No part of this book may be reproduced, stored in a retrieval system, or transmitted by any means without the written permission of the author.

First published by AuthorHouse 03/16/05

ISBN: 1-4208-2673-5 (sc)

Library of Congress Control Number: 2005902479

Printed in the United States of America
Bloomington, Indiana

This book is printed on acid-free paper.

ACKNOWLEDGEMENTS

This book is gratefully dedicated to my husband Don, who has been my greatest fan, and has spent countless hours assisting me.

And, to my mother who spent a lifetime wishing she could write a book.

CHAPTER ONE

The Fire

Jewel sat astride her beloved horse, Lance, as they galloped down the dirt road that would take them home from Coila. It was a cold winter day in January 1932, when Jewel Treadwell had decided to take her horse, Lance, for a ride. Her intention was to just ride for fun. She needed to get away from the house for a while. She had been so overburdened with responsibilities at the gin she felt she needed time to think through all the things that were expected of her. She saddled her horse, waved goodbye to her mother, Berthina, and led the horse down the old familiar dirt road aimlessly going nowhere. She was sure the crisp winter air would clear her head and she could concentrate on her next plan of action. Jewel and Lance had ridden quite a long time and the landmarks told her they had gone about four miles. Suddenly the wind shifted and it was turning colder. It had begun to spit snow, which was an unusual event in Leflore County, and it hit her face like tiny needles. Jewel knew she needed to be heading back to the farm. She pulled up the reins and turned the horse around and headed toward home. By this time she realized how cold it was getting so she urged Lance into a gallop. She hunkered down over Lance, hoping the warmth of the horse's body would somehow soak into her body. Her heavy woolen coat was buttoned to the neck and her hat was pulled down tightly over her ears in an effort to ward off the winter chill. She blinked her eyes trying to see through the whiteness, hoping that Lance could see the road better than she could. The horse knew the way home and she spurred him on in an effort to get there as fast as she could. It would be warm there and a fire would be blazing in the fireplace with a huge pot of soup simmering in the big iron kettle hanging over the coals. She knew the old grandfather clock would soon strike off four, signaling her time to be home or come under the scrutiny of her mother. She never wanted to incur her wrath for something so trivial as being late. Berthina was the worrying type and would wonder what Jewel was up to if she stayed away too long. Jewel was independent and felt she could do without Berthina's constant mothering but she endured her mother's corrections out of respect for her. Since Berthina had become a widow, she was sure that Jewel was all she had left of her own family. Jewel understood her mother's reasoning but still resented the fact that Berthina insisted on controlling her every move.

 As Jewel and Lance were hurrying down the road, she could see a cloud of black smoke off in the distance as she rounded the curve onto the Carrollton road. She wondered just what had caused this ugly sight. It was too big and black to be from the fireplace. As she got closer to the scene, she noticed flames licking higher and higher in the sky. When she and Lance rode closer, she saw it was a large house on fire. Suddenly she realized the awful truth; the fire was at her house. She rammed her heels into the side of the horse, forcing him to run even faster. Jewel could hardly imagine what sight would await her when she got home. When she got nearer to the house she saw fire trucks and horse-drawn fire wagons from all the towns around battling the blaze. It would appear their efforts were futile. The house was completely engulfed in the flames. Jewel wondered if there was anything that she could have done had she been there. The acrid smoke billowed like large black clouds seemingly to cover the earth. It hung heavily in the trees like a moss. The flames licked higher and higher into the night sky. She saw the flames completely reduce her most valuable possessions to ashes. All the things her father had given her, all the books she prized so highly, and even her clothes, were burned to a crisp. She knew some things could be replaced but when the things that she could not replace came to her mind, she quivered at the thought. Jewel could only think of this as one more crisis that she must face. First her father, and now this. The fire was such a disaster the young girl wondered how she would work her way through this one. There would be endless tasks to be done. The farm hands must be fed. She must find a place for her and Berthina to live. And what would they do for clothes? Where would they find things for them to wear? After all she was merely seventeen years old and it seemed almost more than she could comprehend. And yet, she was aware, one more time, the majority of the decisions in this time of trial would have to be made by her.

Immediately, she drew herself back to the present and knew she must bolt into action. First they must all sort through the rubble to see if anything could be salvaged. Before much could be done to clear the mess, they realized the farm animals must be taken care of. She knew Nedra, the cook, would wonder how she could cook and feed everyone with only two old iron pots which was all they had been able to salvage from the ruins so far. Jewel knew this was not the time to dwell on the material things that were lost. She must face reality and think about what she would do now. How could she find a place to live? This was her home. She had been born here in an upstairs room only seventeen plus years before. She had lived all her life in this house.

Jewel was a small girl for her 17 years but she was more grown-up than most kids her age. Her short bobbed auburn hair framed her porcelain like face. The sprinkling of freckles across her nose only enhanced her pixie look. Her flashing green eyes belied what went on in that precocious head. She was small but not frail, young but wise, strong but not arrogant, and deliberate in her decisions. She had proven her strength when she had so ably taken over the management of the gin and the farm when she was just 16. Suddenly that seemed so long ago, even though barely a year had passed. She knew no other world since her life had centered on activities at the farm, at the gins her father owned, or at the church. She had virtually been in control of the gin for a little more than a year now. Her mother had been unable, unequipped, or disinterested in running the business so it fell in Jewel's lap to carry on in the Treadwell family tradition. She had been at her father's right hand most of her life. Now it appeared that she would have to run the business, the farm, and find a place for them to live too. Jewel felt as if she had become an adult in an instant. She was patient and tender with her mother; looking after her when she would have a "spell", which was often. Jewel had always felt Berthina used her feminine wiles to her advantage. She knew her mother had feigned illness to get her way with her father. And it appeared to have worked for her since Harvey was so busy in his own world. He tended to let her win most disagreements just to keep the peace. While Harvey was firm and "in-charge" at the gin or the farm, he sometimes seemed helpless to overrule Berthina or Jewel in their quest for anything. On the other hand, Jewel tried to understand her mother's idiosyncrasies. Berthina was constantly complaining about something. Only Jewel could make her understand when decisions had to be made. If Harvey seemed helpless to control the two women in his life, he had devoted most of his attention to Jewel who was his pride and joy. Harvey Treadwell had spoiled his daughter beyond imagination. If he had ever wished her to be a boy, he never made it known even though he might have felt a male heir would have been more able to succeed him in the business. He had adored Jewel and had always lavished on her all he possibly could. She always had more material things than any of her friends. Her horse Lance was her most prized possession. He had given this beautiful roan when she was very young and she required a large stepping stone to mount him. She promptly named him Lance after a character in a book she had read. The horse stood 16 hands high and it was a long time before Jewel could mount him without help. When she was astride Lance, she felt she was "king of the hill". Harvey had presented the horse to Jewel saying the coat of Lance matched the hair on her head and he knew she would always be in love with fast horses. The saddle for Lance was as good as money could buy. It was hand tooled and made in Italy. It was polished leather with a wonderful patina. It had been shipped to the states on special order from Harvey. Jewel loved that horse more than anything in the world aside from her father. She loved the independence that owning a horse could give her, but she also loved Lance because he was a gift from her daddy. When she was in school at Coila Institute she rode him to school every day tying the horse to the hitching post outside the three-story building. She rode him to the gin after school just as fast as Lance could take her. But now was not the time to reminisce. She had work to do. But, oh, if only she knew where to begin. She would have to look after her mother. And then it came to her; where WAS Berthina? Jewel had not seen her since she had ridden up on her horse and discovered the fire. She was surely with Nedra, the cook, or one of the other hired hands. She found Nedra and was told to look for Sally, her daughter. When Jewel found Sally, she hurriedly told Jewel that Uncle John; Harvey's younger brother and his wife Nancy had taken Berthina home with them. She was hysterical and refused to be consoled. Sally was frantic as she related to Jewel that Berthina had attempted to run into the burning house to retrieve some of her jewelry and clothing when the embers were still glowing red. John had pulled her from the burning building and taken her home with him to attempt to calm her.

Since her mother was being cared for, Jewel decided she needed to handle the problems at hand. For the moment Jewel wondered who was taking care of the farm chores? She felt sure Sam, the overseer, would handle that problem. She paused to wonder how such a fire started? There must be some explanation. Some one said the fire began when coals from the grate fell onto the carpets. Some one else said a farm hand had spilled kerosene on the hearth and it quickly ignited. At this point in time she wondered why it even mattered. Somehow the cause of the fire seemed very trivial at the moment. There were more important things to do now. The fire had been so intense that Jewel felt it would surely burn her brain and she would never be able to think again. But, as she shifted her thoughts into high gear she jammed her heels in the side of Lance and they galloped off down the frozen dirt road going nowhere. She felt a need to think through the problems at hand. She wanted to get away from it all. The wind blew hard against her face as if to blow off the decisions that faced her. The snow had stopped but the ground was covered in a soft white blanket. Everything she saw was white but she could still smell the stench of the smoke from the fire even though they had gone about a mile. Would that awful smell be with her forever? The truth was that she could remember that odor for many years and even in her old age, she could almost bring it back with heavy concentration.

She knew that Lance was getting tired. Suddenly she realized that she couldn't make this poor animal bear her burdens so she reined him in to a short stop. "Running won't get it," she said to herself. Time to pull yourself together and start making some sense of this mess. As they slowly trotted back to the burning embers that was once their home, she began to piece together some of the plans she would have to make. First there would have to be a place to stay. The old cabin down on the front side of the farm where Sam, the overseer lived would do. If the farm hands could clean it up a bit, it would work for tonight. Since there was no food, there would have to be a hurried trip to town to get food for the next day. After all, the farm hands must be fed. They had no clothes or furniture, but that would have to come later. Tonight they would have to make do with what could be foraged from what they had. Nothing had been saved from the fire except a couple of cooking pots. "Well", Jewel thought, "that's a start" "Now, I must go on from there"

As she arrived back at the home sight, she stabled Lance and began to put some plans into action. Since her mother was being cared for, Jewel went to the barn to see what could be done next. She found Sam, and they put together a plan to ready the cabin for them. Sam lived in the cabin, which had been moved to the other side of the farm several years before. Jewel could remember the event of moving the cabin. Her father and the farm hands had winched up the cabin and placed it on logs. They, then, rolled the logs across the field with a team of mules struggling to pull it to the proper resting-place where a foundation of rough-hewn logs had been laid. It faced the road to Carrollton. It had been a difficult job, but Harvey had been determined that the cabin should be in a location that would have a view of the farm that lay to the North. They managed to get it onto the foundation and leveled it as best they could. They hardly expected it to remain for nearly 75 years without changing or remodeling it.

Sam had already sent some of the men to see what had to be done to make it habitable for them for that eventful night. The cook had begun to make a list of provisions that they would need to feed every one in the morning. Jewel found a lot of the decisions had been made and the household seemed to be running rather smoothly in spite of their misfortune. They continued to work far into the night making necessary arrangements. Jewel sent Sally to John's house to check on Berthina and to ask if she could spend the night in their home while she and the hired men continued to make the cabin ready for them.

As the flames began to die down, she could see that there was nothing left of the home-place except ashes and smoke. The fireplace chimneys stood tall and dark as a stark reminder of what once had been and, in the corner, off the room that was once the kitchen, she could see the remnants of her mother's beloved bathtub.

Jewel had gone to the cabin for the night but sleep eluded her. Her mind rambled through the past as she fitfully tossed and turned on the straw tick that had been the bed for Sam. She had assured him it would do for her until better provisions could be secured. Little did she know that she would spend the night thinking of the past? She seemed so young and yet so old at the same time.

She remembered, vividly, her grandparents who had lived in this home and how she loved to play in the huge parlor with them. She quickly brought to mind the times when she heard her "granny" play the old pump organ that sat on the north wall of the parlor. Granny was a wonderful old lady who could do almost anything, at least in Jewel's mind. She could still hear granny singing the old Negro spirituals as she pumped the organ, holding her on her lap at the same time. Granny knew the words to the "marching songs" that were sung during the Civil War and could sing them with the same rhythm as Jewel envisioned the soldiers had as they marched off to war. Jewel never realized that granny could neither read nor write, but she could sing, play the organ, and tell stories that fascinated a little girl. Jewel's grandfather had been a Confederate soldier and fought in the battle of Vicksburg. This Civil War battlefield was not far from the farm. Granny knew all those stories and Jewel was her best audience. Granny had died in the farmhouse and a wake was held in the massive parlor. Neighbors from miles around came to pay the last respects. The farm hands gathered around on the far side of the big room and there was hardly a dry eye in the parlor. Granny was laid to rest in the Black Hawk Cemetery in the family burial plot. Bringing her mind to the present, she realized the old pump organ was now a big pile of ashes and it was almost more than Jewel could bear. Soon a number of memories flashed before her eyes of things that had happened in the old house. She could remember the time her father had installed an inside bathroom for Berthina. She could recall, when she was a small girl, the family had used an "outhouse". One spring, while Berthina was in the old "outhouse", a heavy storm passed through and blew the building down. Berthina was caught in a rather compromising position with her fancy lace "drawers" down around her ankles. She flew into a rage at Harvey insisting that he have one of those newfangled rooms built onto the house that housed a toilet as well as a tub for bathing. He immediately found a man right there in Coila who assured him he could install an indoor bathroom complete with a bathtub. Homer Elshoffer was commissioned to do just that and work commenced on Berthina's new room. When the room was completed, it was a delight for all to see and from that day on, Berthina could almost always be found primping in her new room. Jewel quickly wiped that memory from her mind and drew herself back to the present. As she turned on the makeshift mattress, her thoughts wandered back to the past, again. She had known no other home. Even when she came home for a visit from school, she stayed in her own bedroom. It was her refuge, her hideaway from reality and her mother, Berthina. But that room was no more! This was the home built by her father for his mother. Her father, Harvey, was born in 1881. When he was 5 years old his father died and left a family of 6 boys and 2 girls. They were living in a small house that was bursting at the seams. Harvey determined he would build his mother a home she could be proud of and work commenced on the house in 1900. Harvey and his brothers milled the lumber right on the farm and built the house themselves. Jewel remembered the stories her father had told her of how the timber for the house had been grown on the farm. He told her about what a struggle it was for the hired men to cut the timber and mill it at the sawmill they had erected on the property, and how they worked endlessly trying to lift the large 12x12 logs used as floor joists for the home. The huge two-story house had several rooms but the most important was the parlor that was intended to be the gathering room for all the family. The mere feat of building such a house in that era was just short of a miracle. Jewel could hardly imagine the men being able to do that kind of work. When her grandmother married the second time, she and her new husband also lived in the house and Harvey became half brother to 3 more children. At least one of the Treadwell families had lived in this house since her father finished the house and she had expected to continue the tradition. It had never occurred to her until now that she would not live there until the day she died. Now the cycle had ended. The tradition would have to begin again with her. She was an only child and the heritage would have to continue through her.

Although sleep continued to avoid her, she remembered the times she had helped the cook, Nedra. Their days of hunting greens, the times she helped to build a fire in those same huge fireplaces and her experience of churning milk into butter, all flashed before her eyes. She could remember watching as Nedra hung a pot of soup to cook all day in the fireplace. She remembered the cold winter days when she ran into the house and warmed herself in front of a big roaring fire. She thought about the Christmases when they had gathered around the fireplace in the parlor and shared their gifts with each other. There were always lots of gifts because her father was very generous to his family, and he would make sure that Jewel had everything she wanted. She could remember the times her father brought a newborn calf into the house to warm it by the fireplace so it would live through the cold winter night. She remembered sleeping by the side of the calf all night long, keeping watch over it to relate to her father if anything went wrong. She loved that calf, calling it Moo, and hoping he would let her keep it as a pet. Harvey assured her that no cow could be a pet and she was never told when Moo was the meat on the table. Well, those would all be memories now. She must think of what she would do next. She wondered how she could keep her promise that she made to her father as he lay dying.

Morning came all too soon for Jewel. She had barely slept, tossing and turning in a constant query of the future. She was coming to grips with the loss of all the material things, but she still had a problem with what to do next. She knew that Berthina must be consulted in some of the decisions, but she also knew her judgment was not rational. Berthina was so accustomed to the finer things in life that Harvey had always provided an adjustment to a new level would be difficult to accomplish without a fight. Jewel was in no mood to fight. She simply wanted to get the job done as quickly as possible. Time marches on, she thought, but she must provide a place for Berthina.

They moved into the cabin the next day. Neighbors and relatives came to their rescue by donating household items and furniture. They went about their daily life as normally as possible. Berthina complained bitterly about the conditions in the cabin. She considered it not suitable for her and said so. She resented the fact that there was no running water or bathroom. The thought of taking a bath behind the cook stove in the kitchen was enough to send her into fits. She remembered doing that as a child and vowed never to do that again; however, at this point she had no choice. She was convinced that this whole affair was a big step backwards and she wasn't sure it would be temporary. Jewel, on the other hand, simply took it all in stride and continued to make decisions as they were presented to her. After only a few weeks, Berthina insisted they move to a rent house in Greenwood where Berthina could take a real bath in a real bathtub.

CHAPTER TWO

Berthina

Berthina Foxe was a "wanna-be" society lady. She was a Foxe from Carrollton. Her family had raised her to believe that she was just a "tad" bit better than those around her. She had carried this attitude into her marriage to Harvey Treadwell. He was a "landed" man much like her family. That is to say that he owned a lot of land in Leflore County and the surrounding area. For the most part, the Treadwell family and the Foxe families controlled the county politics and many of the decisions that affected the entire community.

Berthina was a beautiful girl, tall, thin, and well proportioned. Her hair was light in color with a tint of auburn, which she wore in the stylish curls of her day. Because of her fair skin, she must always wear a large hat to prevent those troublesome freckles. She was allowed to powder her nose and even wear a modest blush to accent her rounded features and hazel eyes, but only on special occasions. Berthina was bright but not unusually intelligent. She was not a shy girl, but more probably could be described as audacious. She was a flirt and sometimes stepped over the boundaries of the "well-bred society girl of her time. She dressed in the elegant style of the day and most of her clothes were tailor made for her by the hired help who served her mother. They were always at the height of fashion that was shown in the "Godey" prints in the magazines and rotogravures she saw in the stores. Some of the fabrics used in making her clothes were even imported from England and France by the general store in town that was owned by the Treadwell family. Money was no object when it came to how Berthina looked, as her parents wanted her to marry well. They fostered the idea that she should spend most of her time trying to be even prettier than the other girls from Leflore County. Berthina needed to attract as many men as possible to be able to marry into the right family. Society in Leflore County and Carrollton was limited to afternoon teas, ice cream socials, and country barn dances. Berthina fancied herself above the barn dance scene, but the ice cream socials, usually held on Sunday afternoon, were of a great interest to her. She knew there would always be young men there, and that was where she wanted to be. Many of the young men in attendance she had known since childhood and she found them to be boring. She had a great interest in the "out of towners" that came in from across the river. The Florewood River ran between Greenwood and Indianola. It was a big treat for the young men from Indianola to come to the social events in Black Hawk. When Mt Pleasant Christian Church in Black Hawk had a social, there was always a group from the Christian Church in Indianola. Berthina would don her best dress, her party shoes, and even her white silk stockings to try to make an impression on any one of the boys who came to the party. She would carry her powder and rouge in her handbag until she was near the social, and apply the make-up at the last minute, hoping it would look fresh and not be smeared by the hot, humid weather they were forced to endure in a Mississippi summer. Berthina was very vain and always wanted to look her best in the event an opportunity to meet a man presented itself. It was at one of these socials that Berthina met Harvey Treadwell. She knew who he was because her father and his stepfather had often talked about buying and selling land in Leflore County. She had seen Harvey at church and in their store in town where Berthina's mother and father often shopped for supplies for the farm. She often spoke to Harvey and tried to get his attention but he seemed to be only interested in horses or chicken feed. Her flirtatious, feminine wiles appeared to be wasted on him. She pondered just what it would take to get his attention.

Harvey Treadwell was a hard working, intelligent, shrewd businessman. He was a few years older than Berthina, and had worked in the gin since his father died when he was a boy. He knew how to run every moving part of the gin. He also had worked the farm with the farm hands ever since he was tall enough to walk behind a mule to plow. He was tall and very handsome, strong and muscle bound, and extremely astute in business matters. It was often said of Harvey that he had the brains and brawn of all the Treadwells. There was little doubt in an outsider's mind that these assumptions were true, once you met him. He had very little time for idleness and folly. He prided himself in being very ambitious and he certainly knew the value of a dollar. He had inherited the farm and gin at the death of his father and he was determined to prove himself worthy of his father's faith in him. Even though he was only a small child, Harvey never had in his mind he would do otherwise. Harvey's daily routine consisted of working in either the gin or on the farm. He could not understand any other way of life. Partying was what the idle men did and that was not his style. He had an uncanny ability to handle the hired men and always made sure they were handled with the proper care. However, he was a very firm businessman. His word was the law at the gin or the farm and he rarely had to settle any disputes. He was very successful in his business ventures. Harvey had partners in two other gins besides the one in Black Hawk. One was located in Greenwood and the other in Carrollton. In the eyes of the local business people he was a "home grown entrepreneur". His partners always gave deference to his decisions concerning the business, but it is doubtful that Harvey would have allowed them to speak their mind on the subject anyway. He ran his gins his way and that was the rule of the day.

Girls had always fascinated Harvey but his main interest was in the business. He had entertained lots of girls on the back streets of Carrollton, but none of those floozies would be the one to catch Harvey Treadwell. He was much too smart to lower himself to the ones who had entertained all his friends as well. He would love to have a wife to assist him in all his business ventures but so far, no one had captured his fancy or his heart. He was acquainted with Berthina, but he avoided her when he could, mainly because she seemed too bodacious for him. He was fascinated by her vivaciousness and energy which always controlled the crowd around her, but he also was somewhat intimidated by her. He knew she was a force to 'reckon with, and he just wasn't sure he could handle her. And anyway, he knew she was more fluff than substance. He liked her style, but on the other hand, he couldn't envision her in the kitchen or at the gin. Fate would have another idea for him.

In August, at a church picnic where all the young people of Carrollton and Greenwood were gathered, Berthina was there with her entourage of friends. Mingling through the crowd and obviously looking for the available men she spied Harvey at the food table. He was helping to carry all the food from the wagons to the tables where the spread would be laid out for all to enjoy. She quickly hurried over to him to greet him and make small talk. Harvey was taken aback and continued his chore of helping with the food. Berthina was not to be dismissed. She hung around the table under the shade of the trees until he had finished his job. Then she approached him again, questioning him about his plans for the day. He had none. This revelation aroused in Berthina the hope that she could solve his loneliness. She immediately invited him to join her at the creek bank for lunch. She would bring along a well-filled picnic basket for them to share. Much to her surprise and delight he accepted. Harvey did not enjoy these social functions and he saw her invitation as a way to escape all the falderol of the event.

As soon as they could possibly escape their families, they hurried to the creek for their lunch. Berthina had prepared a huge lunch for them to eat. Their conversations seemed to be about mundane things. She showed an amazing interest in the operation of the gin and that impressed Harvey. She questioned him about some of the land purchases he had made and he fell for that ruse by explaining, acre by acre, just what they had purchased. She feigned an interest in this boring subject but it was enough to fool Harvey.

After the picnic lunch was over and the evening sun began to set, they wandered back to the social. There was work to be done there in cleaning up the spoils of the huge dinner. They went their separate ways to assist their families with the loading the wagons of the leftovers. Harvey asked Berthina if he could see her again soon. Berthina was ecstatic that she would have another meeting with Harvey Treadwell. Suddenly the men from Indianola seemed unimportant to her.

Berthina and Harvey became an "item" that summer seeing each other as often as they could. Her parents and his were overjoyed at the prospect of this happy couple marrying before spring. Harvey accepted Berthina's gregariousness and she continued to be in awe of his business acumen. Not once did she question his ability to make a decision about business affairs, and she was content to simply follow and obey his commands. After all, he was the man of her dreams. Displeasing him was the farthest thing from her mind.

As summer turned into fall, the days got shorter and that was a signal that winter was not far behind. There was lots of farm work to be done and Harvey had to spend most of his time making sure the farm hands worked to complete the harvesting. For the most part, the cotton business had slowed down until winter. But there were many more chores to be done at the farm before winter came. The granaries had to be filled and the hay must be stored for the livestock. Harvey seemed to work non-stop at the farm to insure that all the necessary work was done. One afternoon, Berthina took the buggy to the barn where she knew Harvey would be helping put up hay. He had been there since early morning and she thought she could visit him at the end of the day. As she arrived at the gate, she saw him in the distance, broad shouldered, muscular, and brown. He caught sight of her as she did him, and their eyes met for an instant. She offered him the fresh lemonade she had brought to him and they went inside the barn to enjoy it in the shade. The hay was stacked high and while the air was stifling; the fragrance of the freshly cut hay was intoxicating to her. Harvey invited her to look around the barn emphasizing the stalls where the horses were stabled. Berthina was unimpressed but managed to continue to listen to Harvey extol the virtues of these surroundings. She was completely enthralled in his ability to be so interested in horses and barns. He invited her to climb the makeshift ladder to the top of the loft to view the barn from above. She deftly climbed to the top, holding up her skirts to prevent her tripping on them and at the same time, revealed her white silk stocking and ankles. Harvey took notice of this lovely sight and was quickly aroused. He was not one to shy away from a pretty woman, particularly one so bold as Berthina Foxe. As he assisted her up the ladder and they stood together viewing the horses and tackle below, it seemed natural for him to hold her in his arms. Needless to say, Berthina melted in ecstasy at the thought that she finally had Harvey Treadwell where she wanted him. What happened next seemed only a natural occurrence for Harvey, but completely overwhelmed Berthina. She was not experienced in what to do next, but knew that whatever it was, she would follow his lead. Never in her dreams did she think it would be like this. No schooling, book reading, or lessons from her mother or the hired help prepared her for such an event.

The sun began to set in the west and Berthina and Harvey knew they must get back to their families. As they left the barn Harvey assured her he would call on her soon. Berthina whipped the horse into a trot all the way home, but nothing would remove from her mind the wonderful experience she had just had. As she kept the horses in a fast trot she pondered the event. Even the thought of what had happened aroused her again. What a wonderful man he was, so gentle and patient.

No one would ever hear one word of this from her, not her mother or the other busybodies in town. Harvey Treadwell was hers. She knew it and now she had to figure out how to make it permanent. Little did she know that the Jewel of Leflore County would soon be within her grasp.

CHAPTER THREE

The Birth of a Jewel

Berthina Foxe and Harvey Treadwell were married the following June. It was a very fashionable wedding with all the trappings of a high society event. Everyone who was anyone was in attendance. The cooks had been busy for weeks preparing food for the all day happening. Sally, the cook's daughter, who was an excellent seamstress, had worked for months on Berthina's dress. The fabric had come directly from France and arrived in New Orleans by boat. Her father had sent a hired hand in a buggy to bring it back. The design of the dress came from Paris and featured row after row of seed pearls to be sewn on the bodice. Down the back opening were 36 small pearls with ringlet loops to fasten the bodice in a tight fashion around Berthina's tiny waist. The train of the dress was nine feet long and was a volley of cascading layers of silk peau-de-soile ending with another layer of seed pearls around the hem. The entire dress fit her stunning frame and she appeared to be nothing short of an angel is the creation. Sally had certainly outdone herself on this dress. The hat she had chosen was adorned with more silk tulle and pearls. It featured a large bow on the side made entirely of tulle but featured a large pale pink silk rose, which Sally had designed and placed in the center of the bow. Adding this accent to her hat gave it the air of aristocracy, a fitting tribute to the entire event.

Berthina was a beautiful bride. She was tall and thin and the dress accented her statuesque body. She knew how to carry herself and just how much make-up to use to make her appear more beautiful but not "cheap". Her jewelry was all a gift from Harvey. Her wedding ring had a very large diamond in it and she was sure it had come from Memphis. She knew that Harvey had paid a good price for it. But the cost didn't impress Berthina as much as the size of the diamond and sparkle. Not one of her friends who had married that spring could sport one of this quality. Her single necklace was strand of cultured pearls although she had many things from which to choose. Berthina longed to be looked at and this was her day.

After the ceremony at the Mt. Pleasant Christian Church, a reception was held in the big house at the Treadwell farm. Food was laid out on every table the Treadwell family could locate. It appeared they felt as the disciples of Jesus felt at the feeding of the 5000 during the marriage feast of Cana. Berthina's family was there to help but the Foxe family was somewhat over shadowed by the hustle and bustle of Nedra, the cook, Sally, her daughter, and all of the Treadwell clan.

Berthina and Harvey moved into the family home and lived with his parents. This arrangement suited Berthina perfectly. She need not assume any role other than to remain beautiful. No involvement from her in the everyday routine of the household was required. She could lounge in bed, stay in their room, or wander the gardens to her heart's content. Working or managing had never been her strong suite. She only knew how to manage her wardrobe and to give orders to launder, iron, or make her a dress. Occasionally she would go to a garden club meeting or an afternoon tea with the ladies of Carrollton. She longed for a fancier place in which to hold court, but Harvey was a Treadwell of Leflore County, and she could hardly hope for anything more than this.

Berthina and Harvey had the entire second floor of the farmhouse as their living quarters. They enjoyed the privacy this arrangement allowed them. Harvey was very busy during the day, but he devoted his evenings entirely to Berthina. She spent her day preparing for his arrival and always was receptive to his amorous advances. Berthina loved his manly prowess and sometimes felt guilty that she enjoyed all his methods and manipulations. Sometimes she wondered where he had learned all these things, but in moments of passion she carefully pushed those thoughts to the back of her mind. She had been taught that girls just submitted to the men, but she actually loved being loved. She sometimes wished he could come home during the day just for her. Harvey was always happy to oblige her but often wondered if he was enough for her since she seemed never to be satiated. However, he attended to his "manly" duties with finesse and grace. He was a gentleman and continued to please Berthina in every way he could.

Shortly after their marriage Berthina discovered that she was pregnant. This revelation was not exactly what she wanted to hear.

She had friends who had married and immediately had children. Berthina was not the domestic type although she had learned the finer things of being a southern belle. She knew how to entertain when she was expected to do so. She had learned the art of table etiquette from her mother. She also knew how to organize and give a dinner party for Harvey's friends or just the local literary club. She was an expert at handling the cooks and maids in order to be considered a grand hostess. But being pregnant was another story. She was hardly the motherly type. The thought of getting huge, having a baby spit-up on her, or worse yet, to soil her fine wardrobe was not an event that she was looking forward to. However, Berthina knew it would be inevitable that she would bear children even though she considered it an insult to her vanity. She was concerned about her hourglass figure. This would mean she would become fat and ugly. How could she handle this blow to her ego? Harvey seemed overjoyed at becoming a father, but she found the news depressing. Of course there would be lots of parties and luncheons to celebrate the news, but when she became cumbersome, she knew she would have to hibernate in her room. No one, not even Harvey, would see her in this bovine state ever again.

    Jewel Treadwell was born on September 8, 1914, to Berthina and Harvey Treadwell in the little community called Black Hawk. On the day she was born, the fall breeze seemed to herald in the beginning of another era for the Treadwell clan. The sun was bright and the leaves had just begun to turn their fall colors. Nedra, the cook, had attended to Berthina and helped to bring this tiny redheaded bundle into the world while Sam, the overseer of the farm had sped into town on the horse to get the doctor. By the time old Doc Rogers got to the house Jewel was already bathed and wrapped in a pretty pink blanket. She was trying her best to nurse from her mother's breast. Berthina was not having much success in coaxing the little doll to nurse. Although she seemed to have plenty of milk to feed the hungry child, she didn't have the technique figured out. Nedra came to her rescue and began to work with Berthina and the baby until they managed to get the baby to nurse and stop crying.

Doc Rogers was the neighborhood's doctor who had delivered many babies in Leflore County. He usually rode his horse from house to house checking on the women about to give birth, but Berthina jumped the gun on him and delivered her baby a week or so early. The old Doc was not unnerved by the "midwifeing" of Nedra and he congratulated her on the fine job she had done. He took one look at the child and announced her to be the "Jewel of Leflore County". A prettier baby he had never seen. Harvey Treadwell was so overwhelmed he could barely speak. When he took his first look at her, his eyes filled with tears. Harvey was a burley kind of guy, one who didn't show much emotion, but the sight of his baby daughter was more than he could handle. He quickly left the room to hide his tear stained face. He paced the floor outside the birthing room in silence. His disappointment that the baby was not a boy evaporated faster than his tears when he thought about that chubby little bundle that was his creation. If he felt a boy would follow him into the gin and succeed him in the business, he didn't show it. Little did Harvey know that the baby girl in the next room would show all of the abilities, strengths, and fortitude that any man would have shown toward a business. She would ably succeed him and more, as time would tell.

The Treadwell gins were a flourishing business. Harvey Treadwell employed several of the local people around the community. However, most of the folks around the small community either farmed their own land or rented land from Harvey. If Harvey needed additional help he had to hire men from Carrollton. Even though Carrollton was the nearest town of any size it did not have many businesses that hired extra help. Most of the shops and stores were owned and operated as a family enterprise. Men looking for work need only drop by the gin and ask for Harvey. If they really wanted to work, there was usually a job for them somewhere on the Treadwell farm.

Harvey managed the gins very successfully. Cotton was "King" in the Mississippi Delta area in 1914. Most of the farmers in the area grew cotton as a cash crop. His tenant farmers could grow cotton then bring it to his gin when the cotton had been picked. The market was strong for cotton and a farmer could make enough to feed his family for a winter if he worked hard on his crops. Harvey owned a lot of land and he allowed it to be farmed by many of the local farmers on a 50/50 basis. Field hands were plentiful and most of them worked for little pay as long as they could grow a garden and have a shanty to live in. Many of the wives and children of the farm hands worked in the fields, picking or planting as the season demanded. Others worked in the kitchen for farmers' wives or as nannies for the children. When the cotton was ready to be picked, it took every available hand to bring in the crop. This was always the best time for Harvey Treadwell. It didn't take long to know whether or not he would have a good year or a bad one. Over the past twenty years he had been able to acquire quite a fortune. He now owned about 1500 acres of good farmland. He had about 800 acres of timber that was about ready to be cut. Besides the farm he and "Uncle" Ewing Carlton owned the gin in Black Hawk and he was able to handle the cotton ginning needs for most of the people for miles around. He also owned a general store in the community of Black Hawk. The community got its name from the covey of black hawks that seem to inhabit the area each winter. Harvey's younger brother John ran the store for the family. The store provided the families in the area with needed supplies and groceries. Because it also had a dry goods section, the neighborhood women were able to get the fabric and notions they needed to keep their families in clothing.

Carrollton, a town nearby, was a grungy town. The streets were dusty and dirty. The farm wagons brought to town to procure supplies for the farms seemed to deposit their over burden of dirt or mud as if they were substituting one load for another. There wasn't much business in Carrollton. A general store owned by the Johnson family stood on the northeast corner of the town. On another corner was a drug store where you could buy your arthritis lineament, paregoric to cure the babies' colic, or alcohol to swab out a cut. In the winter you could buy hot coffee at the lunch counter or a cooling chocolate phosphate in the summer for only a nickel. Even so, a nickel was hard to come by for some folks, so business was not brisk in any department. Down the street was a funeral parlor that had been in the Frederickson family for more than 50 years. Many of the Civil

War casualties had been returned to the funeral parlor for burial in the Black Hawk cemetery. All the local folks had been buried there for many generations because there was no other place within miles where loved ones could be interred.

The First State Bank of Carrollton cast a formidable shadow on the town because of its ominous size. The pillars in front served as open arms to welcome any new customers. They also appeared to be reminders of its stability to those whose life savings were on deposit there. However, times were good and depositors were plentiful. The "moneyed" families maintained sizeable deposits so the bank appeared to be prosperous in 1914. Harvey Treadwell used the bank for all his business interests. He not only was a large depositor but a borrower by no small means. The gin and the farm were both mortgaged heavily and he carefully paid on the debts regularly. The proceeds from crops, the sale of lumber, and the general store more than satisfied the debts with plenty left over. But, Harvey was not a frugal man. In fact, he sometimes was foolhardy especially if it was something for Berthina. Whatever Berthina wanted Berthina got, and she knew it.

Sandwiched between the Bank and the drug store was old Doc Rogers' office. It was a small space but inside was room for curing the sick. It was painted a dull white and the furniture seemed to be early "revolution era", or maybe leftover attic! The interior gave the aura of sterility if erroneously so. An examination table was old and a bit rickety, however it served to examine a small child's sore throat or an expectant mother about to give birth. Doc Rogers had delivered nearly all the babies in Carrollton and surrounding communities for 35 years. His reputation was good, having lost very few newborn babies or mothers and absolutely no fathers. Early in his career he had performed some tonsillectomies and appendices but since 1910 he had refused to cut on anyone for any reason. His refusal was related to a botched tonsillectomy on a five-year old girl who bled to death in his arms. No one knew she was a hemophiliac and he knew of no way to stop the bleeding at that time. The loss of this precious life affected him for years to come and he continued to grieve for this one error.

A few other businesses flourished in town. Among them was the local newspaper. Bill Brownell ran the paper and published the local happenings on a weekly basis. (Many of the townspeople felt it was published on a"weakly"basis). He managed to sell enough ads to the surrounding communities to keep the paper operating. He reported the local news, some national news that he gleaned from the larger papers in the area, the births, deaths, and the marriages. Aside from what he reported most of the area had little knowledge of the outside world. The war in Europe was brewing but had not been noteworthy enough to arouse many of the local gentry to enlist in the armed forces. That was soon to change and many of the young men of the area would leave home to fight a war in a foreign country.

Rounding out the business district was old Heber Howard's saloon. The building itself reflected the image of the owner. Rustic was not a fair assessment of the inside. It was thrown together with rough-cut timbers on a dirt floor, which could have been swept to a hard slick finish, if it had the chance. However, most of the debris of the business remained where it was dropped and became fossilized.

A walk through the warped and inadequate door was an offense to the nostrils. Second hand cigarette smoke mingled with the odor of stale beer, overflowing spittoons, and sweat soaked bodies was enough to turn the entire place into a despicable mess. There were no windows. Fresh air was a non-existent entity. The men who patronized old Heber's place never seemed to mind the ambiance. Store bought whiskey was expensive, but there was an unlimited supply of bootleg whiskey in Leflore County, and it could be bought for a pittance. Law enforcement officials turned their heads at the selling of the illegal brew and Heber knew it. Every evening the farm hands from all around Carrollton stopped in for a "cold one" on the way home to their families if they could possibly scare up a dime or two to pay. Those who couldn't pay simply ran a "tab" and promised to pay when the crops came in, or their cotton sold or when times changed. Heber knew that many of these "tabs" would never be paid, but he continued to hand out the refreshments on a daily basis. He knew that for some of the men it was a break to come here and for some it was a delay tactic before facing the wife at home and the onslaught of her daily diatribes about their life (or lack of one). On Saturday night, Heber could count on his saloon being filled to capacity. Fighting and drunkenness was the mode of the day (or night, if you will). Rarely did the fighting become violent but it served as an outlet for the frustrations of poverty and lack of opportunity for betterment. Very few women ever darkened the door and those who did knew that their reputation would be ruined once they crossed the threshold. Harvey Treadwell did not patronize the saloon on a regular basis but knew that most of his hired men did, so he was very familiar with the socializing that took place there. On the night of Jewel's birth, Harvey had no time for "congratulations" at Heber's place. His mind was racing with plans for the future and his new baby daughter.

He wiped the tears from his face, smiled at his good fortune, and stepped back into the room to catch one more glimpse at the newest "addition" to his household. Suddenly he felt as rich as a Rockefeller.

Berthina did not share his enthusiasm. She viewed this squirmy little body as a nuisance and a bother. She could no longer be as "fixy" as she wanted to be. And what of her figure; would she ever be small again? Why must she breast-feed this squally little bundle? Wouldn't that make her rounded, firm, white breast sag? All she wanted to do right now was to fix her hair up in the chignon like it was yesterday before she was beset with all the pain and agony of childbirth. And where was her powder box? Couldn't she at least powder her nose? Why was everyone making such a fuss over this whiny baby? "Oh, Lord", she thought, I have been upstaged!

CHAPTER FOUR

Daddy's Little Girl

From the day she was born, Jewel became the apple of her daddy's eye. Harvey had no experience with newborn babies, but he wanted to cuddle and hold this bundle of joy. Nedra assured him she would not break and carefully showed him how to handle the tiny little bit of his flesh and blood. When she cried, he walked the floor with her talking to her constantly. No one knows what he told her but no doubt it was promises of what the future would hold for her. Jewel was a spoiled baby and demanded that everyone pay attention to her. She wanted everyone to hold her or rock her at all times. Berthina always deferred to Nedra and left the babying to her. They dressed the baby in the finest dresses and bonnets money could buy. She was taken for a walk daily in a pram just like the queen mother of England used for her babies. Nothing that Harvey Treadwell could buy was too good for his little girl. As a toddler, Harvey would have Jewel brought to the gin early in the morning and he played with her during any lull in activities in the office. He taught her how to ride a horse and promised her one as soon as she was big enough to mount into the saddle.

From the time that she was very young, Jewel wanted to be with her father at the gin or on the farm. She wandered around the gin and was fascinated by the machinery. She rode with her father when they got the first gasoline powered tractor. What a wonderful machine she thought it was! When she was big enough to sit behind her father's desk, she tried to run everything. She understood finances better than many of the overseers that Harvey hired. When a farmer brought in a load of cotton, she was always on hand to watch how it was ginned, she tried to count the bales, and as they were being counted she attempted to figure the value. She wanted to help prepare the cotton to be sold. When the money came in, she wanted to help count it and make sure the money and the estimates were the same.

One day, while Jewel was at the gin, her great-uncle Wilbur Foxe came in the building. He was an elder in the Christian Church. He was known as a heavy drinker. He could be seen on the streets of Black Hawk almost anytime under the influence of alcohol. The Pastor of the Christian Church had warned him about his bad habits and had cautioned him that he would be "churched" if he didn't control himself. "Churching" meant that he would be brought before the congregation and disciplined, even dismissed from the flock if he didn't "change his ways". He continued to deny that he had been drinking; he just used his tongue as the cork for the bottle! Quite often he had "corked" too many bottles and would be too drunk to find his way home. Harvey would find Jewel and have her drive the horse and wagon to take Uncle Wilbur home when he was too drunk to get there on his own. Jewel was only five years old, but she was perfectly capable of handling this job for her father. It was about this time that Harvey made good on his promise of getting her a horse. He searched the surrounding counties for the perfect horse for his only daughter. A beautiful roan was purchased in Greenwood and brought to the farm behind a wagon. Jewel was delighted with such a steed even though it required a stepping stool for her to mount him. She rode from the house to the gin, back and forth, several times a day. Berthina didn't like her being at the gin all the time since she was determined she had to learn all the domestic things that young girls were supposed to learn. She made every effort to teach Jewel to embroider or crochet. Jewel resisted all her attempts at teaching her these things. Jewel did consent to be taught the finer points of being a hostess. Her mother taught her to set a proper table. Over and over Jewel heard Berthina say, "the fork goes on the left, the spoon and knife on the right". Jewel learned how to fold the smooth white linen napkins and place them beneath the fork with the fold side out. The crystal water glasses were to be placed above the spoon. All the time she was learning these things she wondered who made up those rules, as they seemed completely backwards to the way she wanted to eat. However she knew she needed to do it Berthina's way if she wanted to eat at her table. And until she grew up she didn't think she would be allowed to change the rules of proper etiquette as they were used in the Treadwell household. In spite of her mother's coaxing, she could see no reason to do domestic handwork. It all seemed like busy work to her and

Jewel would rather be at the gin. Berthina insisted she learn to play the piano, but Jewel had other ideas. Her practicing became such a chore and her mother's patience was so easily chafed that Jewel didn't ever become the accomplished pianist that her mother expected her to be. If it happened at the gin – Jewel wanted to know it, but if it happened at the house, she had no interest in it at all. One exception to her being involved in the affairs at the homeplace was her experience with Nedra, the cook. She would take Jewel with her when they went hunting for "greens". This involved a trip to the field early in the spring where Nedra would look for early shoots of wild edible vegetation. These "greens" included wild mustard, poke, sour dock, lamb's quarter, and other young green plants. Jewel loved these excursions with Nedra and she became so skilled at locating these tender plants that Nedra said she could almost go alone to pick "greens". Not many young girls enjoyed this adventure since it was mostly the hired help that was assigned this chore. Jewel considered any opportunity to go to the field or the woods a big adventure. She would rise early in the morning and wait at the door with her bucket for Nedra. They would fill their buckets with the "greens" and hurry home to cook them for lunch. On one such adventure, Jewel and Nedra encountered a nest of black snakes. It appeared that there were four or five babies and a long, fat one supposedly the mother. Because the mornings were still cool, the snakes seemed lethargic and didn't seem to be bothered by this intrusion of their home. Nedra was deathly afraid of any kind of reptile and immediately began to scream and rant in some unknown language. Jewel ran for the house as fast as short legs would carry her and retrieved her father's pistol.

She approached the nest of snakes and quickly fired the gun several times. She managed to wipe out the mother of the brood and most of the babies, however, one of the babies made its getaway. From that day forward, Nedra refused to go hunting greens without Jewel and "ole dusty" as she called the pistol.

After the hunt for greens was completed and they returned to the house with their bounty, Jewel would stand on a stool by the side of the stove watching how Nedra prepared them. She instructed her in how to clean the greens and that she must wash them several times to "get the snake off'n them" she would say. When it was noontime and the farm workers gathered around the table Jewel could state with pride that she had helped pick them and cook them for their dinner. And of course she would relate the tale of how she had rescued Nedra from near annihilation by slaughtering the family of "vicious" harmless black snakes.

Jewel spent little time at home with her mother, preferring instead to be outside. When it was time for her to go to school she rode her horse to the Coila Academy. Coila Academy was the best school in the area at that time. It was a private school that had been run by a religious group until the State had assumed the role of maintaining it as a State run school. Education was very important to both Berthina and Harvey and the best was hardly good enough for their only child, Jewel. She was eager to learn and surpassed most of the other children in her class. She excelled in arithmetic, a skill that followed her the rest of her life. She also absorbed all the history she could get and was especially interested in the Civil War. There was a battleground very near their home. Jewel visited the site often and carried the horror of that battle with her throughout her life. Her next favorite subject was reading. She loved the stories that the headmaster taught at Coila and upon returning home in the evening she related them to all that would listen, around the dinner table.

By the time she was 10 years old, Jewel was as grown-up as most twenty-year-olds, although her size belied that fact. She had short-cropped hair and her round face featured dimples and freckles, all of which gave her the look of a cherub although her actions sometimes made her cherubic look a sham. Underneath all the feminine "trappings" was a head full of information. Since her young childhood she had been in her father's footsteps almost before he vacated them. She longed for knowledge – about everything. She was a voracious reader and if she couldn't get a book from the book supply at the school she rode her horse into town to the library for a new supply of her favorites. Kate Greenaway and Nancy Drew were her favorite novels, however, she loved the study of Abraham Lincoln. She absorbed all she could about his family and the leadership role he had taken during the Civil War. She kept a list of all the books she had read, hoping to find a new one on each trip to town. She often read the ones she had over and over again. Each time she put herself in the place of the heroine. She climbed rooftops to catch the villain, or trampled through woods to seek adventure. She fantasized that she was Nancy Drew. After reading "Black Beauty" she knew she was the heroine and her horse, Lance, was the title character. She was sure that Lance could do everything that Black Beauty had done. As she read Rebecca of Sunnybrooke

Farm she knew she was not that character, and placed the book on the shelf never to be read again.

Jewel was a loner, preferring the company of the hired hands at her father's business to the girls her age in Black Hawk. Her friends were mostly neighbor girls or relatives and they bored her. Their interest was in dolls and playing house. Although Harvey had purchased for her the prettiest dolls from Germany or Paris, dressed in the finest clothing money could buy Jewel wanted no part of that world. She was a tomboy and preferred riding horses, playing stickball with the boys or being at the gin. Although she played with the children of the hired hands and the boys in the neighborhood, none of them struck her fancy. Even at an early age, she shunned the everyday life that was expected of her. Her life was her own and she kept it that way. Occasionally Harvey would simply run her out of the gin. If he was too busy to watch the ever-moving little girl, she would be left to her own devices. One such day she left the gin and wandered home. She knew about the wellhouse that sat in the far side of the back yard. She also knew it was off limits because Nedra kept the milk, cream and other perishables in there. Under the building was a bubbling spring that was used for the water in the house but because the spring ran deep, it also kept the food stored in the building at a cool temperature. Harvey had given Jewel a black kitten as her own and she was told it would have to stay outside. "Midnight" followed Jewel around the farm wherever she went. On this bright sunny afternoon, Jewel decided to explore the wellhouse. Standing on tiptoes she was able to unlatch the door and go inside. All around the walls were shelves that were groaning with the weight of the crocks of milk and cream. Some of the milk in the back was obviously spoiled but she knew it was used for churning butter. The containers of cream were used for the luscious desserts Nedra made every day. On the top shelves were packages of smoked meat tightly wrapped to keep out the vermin. As Jewel was busy contemplating the bubbling spring she failed to see that Midnight had followed her into the room. The kitten was obviously in "cat heaven" having spied the crocks of milk. She was into each one drinking as fast as she could. The instant Jewel tried to retrieve her Midnight spied a mouse. The race was on! The cat ran, jumping through everything in her path in hot pursuit of the poor mouse. The mouse feared for its life, justifiably so, and jumped into every crock or pan and swam for dear life in its effort to escape. Jewel scampered about the room trying to catch either one of the animals. Milk, cream, and Midnight, the cat, were everywhere. The mouse got away, but not before everything was drenched in milk. Midnight returned to her next love, the meat packages on the top shelf. When Jewel tried to pick her up, she scratched and clawed with her tiny claws on every piece of flesh she could reach before she was thrown bodily out the door. The thought occurred to Jewel she should just drown her in the spring, but she knew Nedra would surely kill her for that. When Jewel came in the back door of the house, her crime was evident. Nedra scolded her and told her if she ever did that again she would give her a "good thrashin". As she stood in the kitchen helping Nedra clean the cream and sour milk from her skin, and dress, doctoring the scratches and admonishing her for her misbehavior, Jewel wondered just how a "thrashin" could be good!

As soon as Jewel could be cleaned up, Nedra decided to give her a chore to do. She could help her churn the butter. Jewel watched as Nedra took the old stone jar from the pantry and poured the soured milk and cream into it. Jewel then was instructed to take the "dasher" up and down until it became butter. Now Jewel wondered about the mechanics of this action but decided she should follow Nedra's instructions. To do anything less would surely arouse her wrath again. Obedience seemed to be the most expedient thing to do. After a short time, much to Jewel's surprise, the stone jar contained butter and buttermilk. Nedra gathered the butter and put it in a large bowl, straining the buttermilk for the last bits of butter, and returned the buttermilk to the wellhouse. Earlier in the day, Nedra had made "light bread". It was a routine she did nearly every day. In the past, Jewel had watched as Nedra took a ball of dough and placed it in a bowl, setting the bowl in the window to "rise". This was a curiosity to Jewel and she wondered how a small ball of dough became a large loaf of bread for supper. At about the time Jewel had finished the chore of churning, Nedra took a loaf of bread from the oven. All was forgiven when she plopped Jewel on her favorite stool and generously slathered a slice of the warm bread with the butter she had just churned, muttering something about a child "gotta be forgiven for the dirt she'd done". Jewel leaned as close to Nedra as she could get and proceeded to eat the fresh bread and butter, all the while muttering something about Midnight being a good kitten and the mouse should not have been in the way. After all Midnight didn't drink much milk anyway.

Jewel had her father wrapped around her finger. She knew "her wish was his command". He never denied her anything she ever wanted. Because she was with him everyday, she rarely asked for much. She had an intense interest in cars and their engines. They simply fascinated her. For her tenth birthday, Harvey gave her a Model T roadster to scoot around town in. She was so short she could not reach the foot pedals so the men at the gin rigged an extension on the brake pedal so her short legs would reach them for control of this new-fangled contraption. She learned to drive her car by manipulating the hand controls. Henry Ford would have been proud to see such a precocious 10-year-old showing off or cruising around Black Hawk in his invention. Jewel loved her car and the independence it gave her. She drove the car everywhere she went when her horse was not the transport of choice.

Although Jewel was fascinated by the invention of motorized vehicles it was a great thrill of hers to invite the newly invented "pickup" truck to a race with her horse. She and her cousins delighted in waiting by the side of the road for the approaching "peddler " in a truck and challenge him to a race. The peddlers drove the new kind of trucks with wooden sides that would hold items for sale. He was virtually a travelling department store. Everything imaginable could be bought from the peddlers. Many housewives did not have a way to go to town in 1925 and they were delighted to have the peddler wagon ramble up their driveway. The woman of the house could get a bottle of vanilla, a new chimney for her coal oil lamp, a copy of the newest "Ladies Home Journal", or five yards of fabric for a new dress from the peddler. He also offered her the latest gossip from her nearest neighbor who might be 10 miles down the road. Jewel knew the schedule for the peddlers and if she could escape Berthina, she would gather up her cousins, mount on their horses and harass the peddler with their racing techniques. Of course, no mention was ever made to anyone as to these antics, but Jewel delighted in the fact that the peddlers rarely won the race.

Jewel attended the Mt. Pleasant Christian Church regularly with her parents. The history of this church stretched far back into the Treadwell family. Her grandfather, Elbert Treadwell had given the land for the church to be built in the late 1870's. From the beginning of the church, there had always been Treadwells in attendance. Harvey and Berthina were no exception. They attended the church as a family regularly. Jewel loved the church and the services that were held there. If there was a service at the church, Jewel was there. The pastor, Hiram Johnson, enthralled her. His sermons based on various stories in the Bible held her interest. The Old Testament was her favorite subject containing the history of Israel and how its stories were prophetic to the New Testament. It read like magic in her mind. She believed every word the preacher said and before long, she was "saved" and asked if she could join the church on her own. Berthina was not in favor of this action, believing instead that she was much too young to understand the meaning of salvation and baptism. Jewel insisted and engaged the influence of her father to convince Berthina. Harvey, of course, stepped in and persuaded her to relent. In 1925, Jewel became a full-fledged member of the Mt. Pleasant Christian Church of Black Hawk, and forever after remained active in the fledgling community church. Harvey

Treadwell was not a spiritual man; however, each spring when the church held its week-long revival meeting, he closed the gin for the entire week. He felt this gave his hired men an opportunity to "get religion". Perhaps he felt this would make them easier to work with at the gin or on the farm. Perhaps Harvey had a spiritual side but he refused to show it on the outside. He certainly was a very grateful man for his many blessing, the least of which was continued success at his business enterprises and his beautiful daughter. He spoke with the pastor of the church on many occasions and reported that he felt he had been blessed beyond all measure. In any case, the week off from the work at the gin was viewed as a vacation for many of the workers, regardless of the underlying reason that Harvey chose to close the gin.

Church activities did not impress Jewel. She wanted the messages and not the frivolity. Her reading and study habits changed drastically after she was baptized and she became a Bible student. She turned her thoughts toward understanding all she could about the Bible and was completely enthralled with her studies and the effect they could have on her life.

When Jewel completed her elementary education at Coila, Berthina felt that she would get a better education if she went to school in Carrollton. Jewel was "shipped" off to stay at a boarding house in town during the winter months, to attend school, returning to the farm in the summer. Whether Berthina wanted to be rid of the burden of handling Jewel or whether she really felt the school was a good idea, will never be known. However, Berthina reportedly stated that it was the happiest day of her life when Jewel packed up and went away to school. It would be reasonable to assume that Berthina thought an education in the Carrollton School would change Jewel from the tomboy she was into a finished lady. Whatever the reason behind the action to send her away for her education, Jewel did not fight going to Carrollton School. She considered it a challenge that she could easily handle. She became a serious student and learned quickly the lessons they taught from arithmetic to history. She loved it all. She missed her father and the gin but her education was important to her so she persevered in all her studies and excelled in everything the school had to offer.

CHAPTER FIVE

The Murder

By 1930 times were growing lean in Leflore County. The effect of the Great Depression was upon them. Many of the farmers in the county were experiencing hard times. Summer brought the worst drought the county had seen in many a year. The "dust bowl" of Oklahoma occurred at the same time and Leflore County did not escape similar devastation. It brought on an adverse effect on the cotton crop as well as the other farm crops so necessary for the family food supply. When the income from the crops was down, so was business at the store. Harvey had to lay off some of the workers causing more hard times for everyone. It had a domino effect. Most of the workers had families and the questions for livelihood quickly were unanswerable. Harvey was hard nosed about his business practices, and he didn't hesitate to fire anyone from a job when it came to his profitability. Harvey knew the value of a dollar and made no bones about firing those men who did not help him make money. Some of the men were hard to handle on a daily basis so they were the ones that Harvey felt he should eliminate first in order to protect loyal workers as long as he could. He, too, was experiencing hard times. His bank notes were due and he was barely able to keep them current. His savings had dwindled almost as fast as the cotton crop. Berthina didn't understand these things and had continued her usual spending habits. When he was at wits end with her, he finally insisted that she refrain from running up any more "tabs" in town for frivolous items and limit her spending to things absolutely necessary for running the household. While Jewel was away at school, she was unaware of the events going on at the gin. She had always worked side by side with her father but he rarely discussed money or the lack thereof with her. Poverty, in her mind's eye was reserved for the hired help and did not apply to the Treadwell family. Little did she know about what the future held.

By the winter of 1930, Harvey Treadwell was down to a precious few workers at the gin. There were still a few hired hands on the farm because they were self-sufficient. Most of Harvey's farmland had been rented out on a 50/50 basis. Richard McLean rented one of Harvey's farms that he farmed for shares in this manner. On a bright sunshiny day in December, Richard McLean, brought some cotton to be ginned. He felt sure he knew exactly how many bales he would have. He was not an educated man, but he had a good knowledge of figures. And he was not a patient man who had a basic distrust for Harvey, as did a lot of the share farmers. He watched everything that took place during the process of ginning his cotton. A bale of cotton weighed between 700 and 900 pounds and represented a lot of money and a lot of hard work. When the ginning job was completed, Richard disputed the amount of cotton that he was being paid for. As usual, Harvey was very firm about the amount he had ginned and he stood his ground. He refused to change the ticket he had prepared for Richard and walked away from him in a most degrading manner. Richard was not to be dismissed this way. He had a short temper and everyone knew he always carried a pistol. He left the gin, walked into the street, and called Harvey's name. When Harvey came to the door of the gin, Richard fired one shot and hit him in the face. Richard left the scene and walked to the town of Redbanks to the Stewart home and asked to use their water to shave. Upon completing the job, he turned to Mr. Stewart calmly announcing that he had just killed Harvey Treadwell. He then, asked to use their phone to call the Sheriff. Since the Stewarts's had no phone, he went on up the road to another neighbor, leaving Mr. Stewart in shock. Richard stopped at the Wilkinson's place and asked to use their phone. He called the Sheriff of Leflore County and repeated the story. He waited patiently in their home for the sheriff to arrive to take him away.

Harvey Treadwell refused to die – calling instead for them to fetch Jewel immediately. She arrived at the gin in time to cradle her beloved father in her arms. His final words to her through his mangled face were that she was now "in-charge". He asked her to promise him she would always "guard the land".

Harvey died the next day. Jewel was nearly inconsolable. She could only think of what she would do without her father. She had adored him and he felt the same about her. There was never a day that she didn't see her father, even when she was away in school, he made a practice to visit her sometime during the day. Jewel couldn't imagine life without her father. It almost seemed a burden too hard to bear. Jewel knew she could not expect any consolation from her mother. Berthina wondered what she would do without his support. While she had loved Harvey, she was more interested in herself and what he had provided for her. But Jewel's heart was broken.

Harvey was buried in the Black Hawk Cemetery. The funeral was the largest the community had seen in a long time. Harvey was well known and a pillar in the community. While he was a stern businessman, the townspeople respected him. His death was to be a tremendous loss to Jewel and to Berthina and to all of Leflore County. Jewel was, indeed, in-charge even though her father had left everything to Berthina. Somehow this didn't seem fair to Jewel, but she was just a young girl and how could Harvey have known this would happen to him. Even with his mortal wound he had enough presence of mind to tell Jewel what to do next. Sadly enough Berthina hardly knew what to do. While she was trying to mourn properly, Jewel was at the gin "taking control".

Berthina, of course, was beside herself. She did not have any idea of what to do next. Life at the Treadwell home was going to change drastically and immediately. Little did Jewel dream at that moment in time that the unfair drama of her young life would unfold with other traumas in the near future.

Jewel didn't know what to do regarding the farm, the store, and the gin, but she knew one thing. If what the preacher at the church said every Sunday was true, and she believed him, then she knew it was time to pray. She wasn't sure she knew how to pray this hurt away, but she went to the back of the farm into the trees and cried till the tears would come no more, then she prayed that God would show her what to do next. Somehow, she knew God had heard her prayers and would answer them in His own way. Then she prayed that she would know His way when there were decisions to be made. She vowed to try to listen for God's plan each day of her life. She promptly stood up and walked briskly back to the house, with the knowledge that she had Divine guidance in her decisions, even if others doubted her.

Very early the next morning Jewel was at the gin going over the books. Payroll records, purchases of supplies, sales of cotton, receipts from the farm, and expenses of the household all had to be reviewed. If in fact she was "in charge", as her father had so plainly stated, she wondered if she would have to prove it to anyone. Lord knows, Berthina couldn't do it as she had not been to the gin more than three or four times in her life. Uncle Ewing Carlton had been Harvey's partner in the gin. But Jewel was not about to step back unless she was forced to and not even then without a fight. As she sat at the desk looking over the state of affairs, she realized that she would never go back to school. She sent Sam into Carrollton to get her possessions from the boarding house and from that day forward she would become self-educated. Jewel never looked back with regret.

CHAPTER SIX

Jewel in Charge

What Jewel saw in the paperwork before her was not a pretty sight. She saw more red ink than black. The bank account was still intact, but the notes were overdue. The income from the farm in 1930 was negligible, and the sales of cotton were slim. If the spring cotton crops were good this year, she would probably pull the gin out of the red. The farm crop promised to be better this year than last, but there was no guarantee that it would be. But, the most pressing problem was a low cash flow. She knew the only way to raise cash was to sell some of the land. Many of the farmers in the area were as destitute as the Treadwells but there might be one or two who would be interested in buying some land. And what of their timber, she thought. Maybe she could sell some of that.

When Uncle Ewing arrived at the gin with Sam they were astounded to see this petite 16-year-old sitting behind the humongous desk in her father's chair. If she was surprised at their faces, she didn't show it. She began to discuss the financial problems as if she had always been in this chair. They may have had an inkling of the situation but Harvey never discussed his business with anyone. When she mentioned to them that they might need to sell either land or timber, both of them assured her that Harvey would never sell his land. If she heeded their admonition, she would need to pursue the idea of selling timber for needed cash. This was a decision she would handle later and she quickly pushed it to the back of her mind.

While Berthina was in a poor emotional condition because of Harvey's death and the other events taking place at this time, Jewel felt she could do nothing for her. In fact, Jewel had little sympathy for her mother since she, herself, felt the pain of her father's death immensely. Jewel felt she was much closer to him than her mother was and wondered if Berthina just felt the loss of a meal ticket rather than the loneliness that had already beset her. Jewel determined to leave the household for Nedra and Berthina to handle the best way they knew how. She had to tell Nedra that the allowance for the household had been scaled back and she needed to conserve all she could. Jewel felt a pang of guilt because she knew Nedra had always been ultra-conservative in her spending. She didn't want to explain to Nedra why their finances had changed because she wasn't sure herself what she could do to change their financial status. Right now she didn't want to explain anything to anyone. And she also knew the cook was more knowledgeable of the problems than she would ever tell. Jewel felt sure Nedra would heed her warning and conserve all she could in her efforts to be a help to the household. She told Berthina that the spending needed to cease for things that weren't of an absolute nature. Berthina did not challenge Jewel's decision. She was in no condition to handle anything controversial at this point. Jewel thought about the dilemma that faced her and knew that resolutions to some of the most pressing problems needed to be settled and soon! The first item of business was to make sure the gin and the farm continued to run as smoothly as possible. She was sure the farm hands would not respect her decisions or even listen to her point of view. She didn't feel equipped to handle them or their problems. Sam would continue to do his best with the farm. That was her first decision; leave him alone and let him do his job. The next item of business was the running of the gin. While Jewel had first hand knowledge of the business, the hired hands would resent a sixteen-year-old in command regardless of how grown up she might think she was. She opted to have Uncle Ewing continue to run the gins since he was a partner in the business. The last decision she was forced to make on such a short notice was the handling of the income and the outgo. She was adamant that she would assume that role. Maybe that's what Harvey meant when he left her in charge. It didn't matter now, that is what she intended to do. Much to her surprise, Uncle Ewing did not contest her taking on the job of financial manager. Perhaps he knew her better than she thought, or maybe he knew it would be a useless fight to even try to persuade her otherwise.

 For several weeks on end, Jewel arrived at the office long before anyone else. She needed time to think and to be positive that what she saw was fact. She needed to be absolutely convinced that the finances were as grave as they appeared to be. She went to the bank in Carrollton to discuss any alternative method of paying on the notes before they became a more serious problem. (She really avoided the word "FORECLOSURE".) The banker was cordial, but condescending to her. He acted as if he felt she was incapable of the job she had tackled and urged her to leave those decisions to someone more mature. Jewel was enraged at being treated in this manner by someone she wanted to trust. She thought she was mature! While she would have respected his opinion, his attitude so infuriated her that she could not hear anything else he told her. Jewel knew she was young, and her size indicated to most people that she was still a child. However, she knew the head on her shoulders was wise beyond the years on the calendar. Immediately she made a decision to seek other counsel. If the problems were too awesome, she needed to know from someone not attached to the bank or the gin.

Her father had often talked about a man named Stanton who was a fledgling attorney in Jackson. It seemed so far away and she wasn't sure just how to get there, but she knew that Harvey had trusted his judgment. He was only a few years older than Jewel, but if Harvey trusted him then it was inevitable that she should do the same. But, how would she get to Jackson without arousing suspicion in the family? If she was gone for an extended period of time, wouldn't the family wonder about where she was? Harvey had purchased a new pickup truck not long before he was killed, but Jewel had only ridden in it once or twice. She was befuddled over its ability to just move right along with all that horsepower. She knew how to drive her Model T but she wasn't so sure about driving her father's new pickup truck. Maybe Uncle Ewing would show her how to drive it.

She really needed to know. The reasons behind her learning to drive that truck must remain a secret until she felt confident enough to make it into Jackson on her own. It was a long way to Jackson. She had heard her father say it was about 65 miles. That translated into a very long journey in Jewel's mind. Fortunately, she was not easily dissuaded when it came to overcoming obstacles in her path.

After a considerable amount of cajoling Uncle Ewing agreed to teach her to drive the truck. The lessons began in early afternoon. She hurried from the gin to his house, where they kept the pickup, on her horse. Alighting from the horse into the truck was an experience in "bridging the gap" to a different world. Jewel knew instantly this was the "New World" for her. Learning to drive was a piece of cake and she soon drove the truck to town every day for supplies insisting on doing the shopping for Nedra and the household. Using the truck to run these errands gave her the needed experience to go to Jackson on her own. Soon she would have accomplished her goal and off she would go. Her mission was one of necessity and she was filled with excitement at the prospect of going to the BIG city on her own.

Jackson was a big and awesome place. Somehow she hadn't given much thought to what she would do or how she would find Mr. Stanton. She had asked a few questions in Carrollton, but when they gave her street names and buildings, the information was incomprehensible to her. She knew she would have to experience it on her own. She forged ahead without looking back, and soon found the downtown portion of town. Among lots of big buildings, she wandered into a bank, feeling secure in asking questions of the bankers. Of course, they knew who Charlie Stanton was and gave her explicit directions on how to find him. No one asked why such a young girl would need to see Mr. Stanton, and she was prepared to tell anyone some story about him being a relative. However, she never needed to tell anyone that lie.

Charlie Stanton was a very young lawyer. He had only been practicing about three months when Harvey Treadwell was killed. Charlie Stanton's uncle, E.B. Stanton had been a practicing attorney before him, and was now the mayor having retired from practicing law. Charlie wanted to follow in his uncle's footsteps. He had met Harvey through his uncle E.B. but had only talked with him a few times. Harvey had expressed confidence in Charlie and felt he was going to be very successful after he had been practicing awhile. That seemed good enough for Jewel.

Seated behind a large but simple desk was a young man perhaps five or six years older than Jewel, but looking very sophisticated. Here was the man she had longed to see. If she was surprised at his youth, she didn't consider it a problem. She plunged right into conversation with him as if they were old friends. She didn't bother to tell him the events that brought her to Jackson but immediately began to discuss the details of what she needed from him. He knew the circumstances of the family business from his friendship with Harvey, but it was a shock for him to think that a 16 year-old girl was now running the business. However, he would soon have no doubts about Jewel's ability to do so.

Jewel spilled out her story to him, being cautious not to tell any family secrets and carefully guarding the severity of the financial situation. Charlie Stanton was not to be fooled. He knew. She then began to ask about selling land or closing the gin or whatever would satisfy the immediacy of the problem. He assured her he would contact the banker in Carrollton and try to work out some of the problems. Charlie Stanton knew that Harvey would not want to sell his land, but he also knew that he would not want to lose it either. At this point in time there didn't seem to be much of an alternative plan.

Jewel left his office with the assurance that something would be done and soon. If she was naïve about the seriousness of the situation, she didn't show it. She had confidence in her new attorney, regardless of his age or lack of experience. Mr. Stanton was now her friend, as Harvey would have wanted him to be. Her biggest challenge for the moment was to find her way back to the farm before dark.

CHAPTER SEVEN

Jewel Meets Ward

After Jewel had met with Charlie Stanton she felt a little more secure in handling some of the financial affairs. He had assured her that he would discuss her position with the Carrollton Bank in an effort to gain a little time. He knew she would have to sell some the farmland to meet the demands of the Bank, however, he wasn't sure just how serious the situation would have to get before Jewel would allow the land to be sold. He also knew that he had impressed her with the fact that he could be trusted, both with her "secret" of their dire straits and with his ability to handle the affairs of the family.

Her father was right. Jewel had felt very comfortable with Mr. Stanton and knew he would have the best interest of the Treadwell family in any decisions he made. She remembered him telling her that while Harvey would not like to sell the property, he would not want to lose it either. Her next challenge was to convince Berthina that they must sell some land or lose it all. That would not be easy.

Jewel met with Berthina early one morning. She had realized that if you wanted to discuss anything with Berthina it had to be before she had a chance to go to town. Berthina's method of coping with the problems was to go to some event in town. Jewel took a completely different attitude in that she felt you must solve the problems first, then go to town. Jewel had singled out several parcels of land that she thought one of the neighbors might buy. She wasn't sure what she could get for it, but she intended to start high and come down in price if it became necessary. When she approached Berthina with the idea of selling a parcel of land, Berthina was more than willing to sell. She knew their money was running low, but she had no idea just how dire their needs were. Jewel contacted the farmer nearby to see if he would purchase a plot of 100 acres that lay to the North of his farm. He offered her a ridiculously low price, thinking he could get a bargain. He had assumed that the family was destitute or he thought Jewel wouldn't know the value. Whatever the reason, after Jewel had contacted Charlie Stanton, she informed the neighbor the price would be about twice what he was offering. He began to bargain with her and they finally settled on a price somewhere between his offer and Jewel's acceptance. The piece of ground was sectioned off and Jewel accompanied Berthina to the Carrollton Bank to complete the sale. When the bank completed the transaction, he handed Berthina a check for $17.00. She flew into a rage. She had expected the full amount of the purchase price. She had no idea the notes at the bank were so much in arrears. Jewel was a bit surprised herself, but she knew their finances were in trouble. She wondered how many more acres she would have to sell before they would be out of debt completely. Berthina left the bank and climbed into the pickup truck with Jewel for their short trip home. It was not a pleasant trip. She continued to blame Jewel and Uncle Ewing of mishandling the money. She couldn't believe the bank would take all her money in that manner. At that moment she determined she would sell nothing else. Of course, she had no alternative method of making money to support herself and Jewel. She wasn't sure how the hired help would be paid, but she didn't want to agree to sell anything else. Jewel was stymied with her mother's attitude. She knew that something had to be done. Mr. Stanton made it perfectly clear that the land must be sold. Time to pray!! Jewel headed to the woods to commit this problem to the Lord. She prayed for "Divine Guidance" and for the wisdom to know it when she saw it. There was never a doubt in Jewel's mind that she would have a revelation to solve this dilemma.

The business at the gin was nearly over by the spring of 1931. Uncle Ewing was handling the business at the gin the best he knew how. However, the handwriting appeared to be on the wall. They simply had no business. No one had the money for seed or cotton. No one was planting anything indicating that the business at the gin in the fall would be nearly nothing. Uncle Ewing never knew if the business had come to a halt at the Treadwell gin because of Jewel or if the landowners simply didn't have cotton to sell. Did the neighboring farmers consider her unable to do the job, or if the business just wasn't there? Uncle Ewing had been a partner with Harvey prior to his murder. He had never had a specific job. He seemed to have the knack of being available when someone needed his assistance. He had helped train horses for various farmers in the area. He had helped farmers build barns or add a room to their homes for their expanding families. Many men brought their prized bird dogs for Ewing to train. His ability to train even the most difficult dogs was unsurpassed by anyone in the Leflore County. He was a practical joker and no one escaped his sense of humor. Wherever he went he could be depended on to be the life of the party. His ability to handle the business at the gin was a boon to Jewel. At this time of year, they were readying the gin to accept the cotton that had been planted. The machinery all had to be repaired and refurbished before they could accept more cotton to be ginned. Ewing could handle these problems without any input from Jewel. The gin had brought in very little money in the fall of 1931 and the farmland was being readied to plant the crops for the spring of 1932. Everyone was hoping for a good year to help pull them out of the financial fix they were in. Unfortunately it appeared the gin was on its last legs.

After the fire of the home place, the family, being Berthina, Jewel, and Nedra, with her daughter Sally, lived in the cabin on the farm for just a few weeks. They then moved to a rent house in Greenwood. It was a good time to move since they were repairing and overhauling the machinery. There were many farm hands available to help them move. It was not a difficult move now, since most of their prized possessions had been destroyed in the fire. What they had to move was sparse since neighbors and family members had donated it all to them. Jewel did not want to move to town. She loved the cabin, but Berthina insisted they must move away from the farm and the scene of the fire. In spite of the fact they had moved about eleven miles down the road, Jewel spent every-waking moment at the gin for lack of something else to do. She had an innate desire to learn all she could about the operations of both the gin and the farm. Somehow she felt if she understood all she could about the operations that would give her wisdom to save the business. She was approaching 18 now and she considered herself a grown-up. While Berthina would have preferred her to become a socialite, Jewel preferred the life in the business of her father. She avoided those socially correct teen-agers with whom she had attended school, and continued to be at the business more often than in town. On Sunday, she faithfully attended the services at the Mt. Pleasant church, but hurried home as quickly as possible to ride her horse or to drive around town in her car. She really disliked the mundane life of Greenwood and much preferred the company of her horse or the farm hands, or the gin workers to that of anyone else.

One of the young men in Black Hawk was a man named Ward Frederickson. He was born in early 1912 making him about 2 years older than Jewel. He was not sophisticated, and was very worldly in his behavior. He knew all about the back streets of Carrollton as well as Heber Howard's place. He was a frequent visitor of Heber's on Saturday night. He had often squired one of the saloon girls home after hours and the question remained about how long he stayed. He knew, however, that Jewel was a "nice" girl and to win her affection, he would have to put up a good front. He would have to convince her that his intentions were honorable.

Ward Frederickson didn't like to work at anything except repairing a car. His family owned a car repair shop in Greenwood.

His uncle owned the funeral home in Carrollton and Ward could have worked there, but that was not his "cup of tea". He gave lip service to working there but only because he wanted to be the one who drove the ambulance to accident scenes. He wanted no part of embalming dead bodies or even removing a corpse from the deathbed. He was elated when his uncle purchased a 1929 Cadillac hearse. The idea of driving at to speed of 60 miles per hour filled him with excitement. When he could escape his uncle's watchful eye, he would drive around Carrollton and dream of the day he could own a car and it wouldn't have to be a hearse. Even though his father worked on cars, having a car of your own was not commonplace. Ward was sent to the scene with the new ambulance when there was a serious accident in Black Hawk. A car hit a horse that old Doc Rogers was riding. Ward drove the ambulance to the accident scene and helped old Doc Rogers into the machine. The accident occurred just west of Harvey Treadwell's place. He had rushed the Doc to a hospital in Indianola, and the Doc survived. The speed the ambulance could do filled Ward with wonderment, and he was amazed that he could fly that fast and still control the machine. He could hardly wait until the day when he could have such a fast motorized vehicle all of his own.

Because Ward refused to go into the business with his uncle he worked occasionally for his father in the Frederickson Garage. However, that work did not pay enough and he was forced to seek other gainful employment. No one was hiring much in Carrollton or Greenwood but he was able to convince Uncle Ewing Carlton that he could repair the machines at the gin. Ward worked almost daily at the Treadwell farm or the gin. He was very mechanically astute so he was able to repair the gasoline-powered machines at the gin or the farm equipment when it broke down. In many instances, he foresaw problems and could prevent major breakdowns before they happened. Ewing recognized this talent in Ward and thought him to be an asset. At least he felt that way until he found that Ward had just taken the day off for no reason except that he wanted to do so. Ewing found this behavior to be mind-boggling. How could someone who had nothing be so irresponsible? Ward seemed to have no drive to work but he was loaded with charm. He always had an excuse for his absence and Ewing accepted his frivolous stories because he was so good with the machinery. Needless to say, the machinery was fragile and required almost daily repairs. Ward was the best they could find to keep the machinery operating. He knew he was a valuable asset to Ewing and felt he could take advantage of him. Besides, Ward had other interest at the gin. He had his eye on Jewel. He fancied himself as a bit above the common laborers, but had to work in the gin because he had no other income. His family was not a "landed" family and it was necessary for him to work for a living even if it was at a laborer's job. He much admired the vixen of a redhead that sat behind the huge desk in the office and attempted to make decisions with Ewing. She had a level head on her shoulders, he thought, but he knew she kept her eye on the workers who came in the office. She ruled the office with an iron hand and kept her distance from the men who wandered in an out of the gin all day long. These men did not impress Jewel. She was all business when she was behind the desk.

Jewel was a stunning young woman, always-dressed in riding breeches, and shirts, but even then, she cut a dashing figure. She kept her auburn hair pulled back in a short roll that graced the nape of her neck. Most of the men who came in and out of the gin were aware of her sensuality and commented to each other that someday someone would ride away with Jewel. However, none of them felt they would be the lucky guy, except Ward. He continually told them, he would be the one. Time would soon tell the answer to that story.

Ward kept his eye on Jewel. He observed how she handled the affairs at work. He knew very little about girls who could handle themselves in a business setting. His experience was with the local girls at parties. Their limited interest span had been enough to always satisfy his curiosity. He had never felt a need to delve any deeper into the woman psyche. Jewel was a different "breed of cat." She was self-assured; or at least he thought so. She was confident in her every move. She had little time for mundane things and continued to be the force behind the business at the gin. She even held her own place with the farms hands when a hard decision needed to be made. He also saw her as a "force to reckon with". Her ability to make decisions and enforce them firmly took him by surprise. Most men listened when she spoke and they knew her word was law at the gin, including Uncle Ewing. He may have thought he was the boss, but everyone knew Jewel was the "man in charge", and Ewing worked for her.

Ward had in his mind that he would find a way to spirit Jewel away from all this. He thought there might be money to be had in the Treadwell family. He didn't know that Berthina had inherited everything when Harvey was killed. So, in fact, the money had to come through her. And he was unaware of the financial status of the gin. But he was aware that Berthina didn't like him and resented his association with Jewel. While Berthina took no active part in running things, she was aware of the personnel at the farm and the gin. She just had bad feelings about Ward Frederickson. Maybe she had some insight and it would be borne out in the future!

Jewel would never admit to anyone that she enjoyed the attention that the men gave her. But deep down inside she had a strong desire to be courted by a man. She entertained the idea of a man in her life although she was coy. While she wasn't openly a flirt, she would sometimes smile with a twinkle in her eye that suggested that there was more behind that red head of hair than most men knew. She had watched her mother play the flirting game and it sometimes annoyed her. And she failed to recognize the same trait in herself. Jewel was still very sensitive about her father's death and she resented her mother recovering from her mourning so soon. She didn't see her own flirtatious ways as any threat to anyone.

Jewel longed for a male influence in her life, but she wasn't sure it was Ward Frederickson. Since her father died she had no one to talk to about her life or the business. Because she had always been at the center of her father's world, she missed the attention he gave her. Berthina was too busy playing the part of a grieving widow to notice how lonely Jewel was. She failed to see that Jewel was grieving too. When Jewel could find time away from the demands of the gin or Berthina's watchdog eyes she slipped away to meet Ward somewhere. She knew all about his background, his lackadaisical work habits and his affinity for the women at Heber's place, but she was drawn to him like a moth to a flame. He was exciting and he made her laugh. She certainly needed a bit of humor in her life. He continued to encourage her on how she handled the work at the gin. She fed on his attention. A girl of 18, who had such awesome responsibilities, was bound to be easily swayed by the attention lavished on her by anyone. Ward was the "man of the hour". The times they spent together consisted mostly of "shop talk" and plans for the farm as well as the gin. She saw him becoming more and more amorous. While she was wary of his action, she loved every minute of it. It aroused feelings that were very unfamiliar to her and she was unable to comprehend. However, she continued to resist his advances, preferring instead to keep their relationship on a friendly basis. She was not ignorant of the existing situation between them; however, she felt she needed to concentrate on the businesses she was running. Romance was not in her plan but she was having a difficult time keeping it out of her life. The more she saw of Ward, the more she wanted to see him. She wondered if he would work himself into her plan and if so, how soon?

Jewel continued attending church on a regular basis and felt her faith was all that was bringing her through the events of the day. She was able to convince Ward that he should be attending with her. While the community was not aware of their relationship, she felt it was innocent enough to convince him he should seek the Lord. Ward humored her and attended church on several occasions, even participating in the fall picnic on the second Sunday in September.

Ward checked out all the other girls who were at the picnic and spent little time with Jewel. If Jewel noticed this faux paux on Ward's part, she didn't make note of it, preferring, instead to relish the attentions of all the other men at the picnic. She never wanted for male companionship at these church events. She enjoyed the picnic, the service, and all the attention she received from the other men in attendance, even if Ward ignored her.

Jewel could not deny that she was attracted to Ward. She noted his form and physique. She saw his dark hair and seemingly black eyes as dashing. He was tall, slim, muscular, and handsome. He dressed better than most of the men she knew and he had a swagger about him that made Jewel take notice! While she would not admit she was interested in Ward, she made herself available for conversation each time he came into the office at the gin. One late afternoon Ward approached her to ask if she would like to go horseback riding with him after work. They could ride to the creek and watch the evening sun begin to set. Jewel liked the idea of a respite from the drudgery at home. She was weary of hearing Berthina's complaints. And it seemed that all Sally could do was carry-on about her daily routine of handling Berthina.

As they rode together, Ward on his horse, and Jewel on Lance, they laughed at what they saw. The covey of quail they had roused, the late blooming Black-Eyed Susan's nodding their lazy heads as the horses thundered by, and even the dust trail they left behind. It was a carefree time for both of them. Ward was burdened with his family's financial problems that seemed to be never ending. He had to give part of his meager earnings over to his father to help support the family. Ward had a sister at home named Edna, who was four years younger than he. He felt sorry that she had so little. His money problems were not much different from the ones that Jewel was experiencing. Jewel was burdened with the finances at the gin and the household problems too. Her money was running out, and she hated the atmosphere of petty complaints and whining at home. Ward could certainly empathize.

They reined in at the water's edge and spent their time just talking, mostly about the things that happened in their everyday world. However, there was a bond between them that was somewhat electrifying. No mention was made of anything other than a good horseback ride, but there was an underlying feeling they both felt as they talked far into the evening. Darkness was coming too soon for them and they suddenly realized they would be expected home by now. If they didn't hasten to go home, surely someone would be sent to find them. The ride home was less than leisurely as they spurred their horses to a dead run to beat the setting sun. This event would be repeated many times in the near future.

Arriving at the back door, Jewel was greeted by an irate Berthina. She seemed more concerned that Jewel might have an interest in a man than the fact that she was late. Berthina disliked being alone, and yearned for a man in her life. After all, she certainly wasn't an old woman and had worn her widowhood the appropriate time. She hated it, but she knew she must be respectable about it or the community would shun her. Most of the town knew that she would find a man as soon as she could honorably do so. She had just begun to go out socially and was ever on the lookout for someone to end her loneliness. When Jewel mentioned that she had enjoyed her afternoon with Ward, Berthina flew into a rage and forbid her to even think of consorting with the likes of Ward Frederickson. He was penniless and of poor breeding stock. How could Jewel stoop so low as to be seen with him? Jewel could have the pick of the "litter" so to speak. Surely she wouldn't pick so lowly a specimen as Ward. Jewel gave no answer. Her thoughts were that none of the other men in her life filled her with the excitement that Ward did. Most of the men at the church were looking for domesticated women who would work at home and raise children. Jewel had other ideas. She wanted no part of that world, and said so. Her idea of a life was not at home in a house on the hill. Reading voraciously as she did, she had read about all the "far away places" and dreamed of being there frolicking on the beach, or climbing the mountains to see what was below. She longed for adventure. She knew there was more to see outside of Leflore County. She remembered hearing her father talk about trips to New Orleans. That seemed like a fairy tale to her. She wanted to know what was beyond the horizon, to experience the things she'd not had the opportunity to see. She longed to see New York, Denver, even the nightlife in Jackson. It all intrigued her. When would she get away to realize her daydreams if not soon? It was hard for her to realize she was only 18 and the future would be a long time. Jewel wanted the future now. She wanted to leave the dreary life she was leading behind. If she married someone and stayed in Greenwood she foresaw that kind of life as stifling. She couldn't even imagine being in the social scene of afternoon teas, garden luncheons, and sewing circles that abounded in town.

Heaven forbid! On the other hand, times were hard and Jewel knew there would soon be no money from the gin or the farm. She wasn't sure how she would survive when the financial well had gone dry.

Well, Berthina was wrong. Jewel would not succumb to that sort of life and she would need to figure a way around her mother's domination. If she couldn't see Ward in the way she was accustomed, she would invent methods to see him away from her Mother's prying eyes. She wanted to be with him and she would figure out ways to meet him often. He was the best thing she had in her life at this time.

Jewel knew she must continue to unravel the mess she had found at the gin and she felt she could not depend on her own ingenuity to solve the financial problems. Even though she longed to leave it all behind, she was aware that she, and she alone, must continue to do the best job that could be done. She wondered if that would be enough. She also knew Berthina would not be a help to her and she was afraid to trust just anyone. She had confided in Ward some of the problems she had unearthed. He seemed sympathetic to the situation, but was helpless to assist her. He didn't possess her business sense and only listened because that appeared to be what she wanted him to do. Jewel did not see this shallow obedience in him and continued to reveal the problems she faced. Somehow she thought he might have an answer. Ward had the answer, but it wouldn't be the right one.

Ward was not to be dissuaded. He wanted to court Jewel openly, Berthina be damned! He often talked of spending more time together; even suggesting they could go to Jackson together. The opportunity enticed Jewel but she delayed in making that decision. One thing she knew for sure; Ward was not a patient man. Jewel knew there had been many girls in his life, and she often wondered just where she fit in the scheme of things. Jewel didn't know about being jealous, yet she cringed when she thought about Ward being with someone else.

One afternoon they went to the creek and sat on a log near the water. After skipping stones for a while, they settled back to their usual conversation. Suddenly, Ward, grabbed her in his arms, pressed her body to his and kissed her longingly. Jewel was startled but pleased. She didn't bother to push him away, but submitted to his advances willingly. Quickly she came to her senses and realized how much she enjoyed his kiss. She hoped he would do it again, but she tried to play hard to get. After all, a lady was not supposed to enjoy this type of behavior. She assured him that he shouldn't do that again, and before she finished the sentence, he grabbed her the second time and kissed her even more passionately. Suddenly, Ward realized she had returned his advances. He immediately confessed his passionate love for her and he proposed to her, begging her to marry him as soon as possible. She pulled herself away and ran to the pickup truck and tried to open the door to get in and away from giving him a response. Ward quickly came to the side of the truck and apologized to her for his rudeness. Jewel lied and said it was not anything to worry about knowing she would think about little else for days. She needed to decide just why she felt so good and so bad at the same time. She loved the thrill of Ward's kisses, but she knew he was the "forbidden fruit". As Jewel pondered the events that were happening to her, she pushed her conscience to the back of her mind.

Times were getting harder and Ward was no longer working at the gin. He occasionally earned money when he helped out at the funeral home or helped in the Frederickson Garage and that seemed to be enough to support him and his fancy lifestyle. When he completed an ambulance run, quite often he drove the hearse around town with a smug look on his face at his good fortune of being able to drive a motor vehicle. He often took Jewel for a ride in the hearse. They would drive to the creek and climb into the back of the hearse, using it as a hideaway for their courtship. Jewel knew that if her mother ever heard of their escapades in the Frederickson hearse she would go into her one of her tirades against Ward. Jewel, in her innocence, felt she loved Ward, but knew Berthina would have a conniption fit when she informed her of his proposal. Jewel shuddered to think what she would say. She didn't fear Berthina's wrath as much as she wondered what her father would think. Would he be pleased or would he feel the same as Berthina? Harvey had been protective of Jewel but she was only a child. Now she was a woman and her life was taking a turn forsomething beyond the drudgery of the gin. And what of the towns' people; what would they think? Well, Jewel Treadwell had once heard a phrase that said if you have enough courage, you didn't need to worry about a reputation. Jewel Treadwell was never short on courage!

CHAPTER EIGHT

The Trial

Jewel and Ward saw each other as often as they could, defying her mother's command that she shouldn't see him at all. Jewel cautiously kept Ward's proposal from her mother and continued to encourage his advances. They were seen at most of the summer's functions at the church and even in Carrollton at the ice cream socials. Berthina ceased to complain about Jewel's behavior since she, herself, was very busy being courted by various men in the community. She was actively searching for another husband. It was not her nature to be alone, and she planned to obey her inner demands for a man. Berthina was still a beautiful woman. She had a striking figure defying her age and childbirth. She certainly did not look her age. While she was approaching 40, she still maintained a youthful beauty thanks to all the cosmetics that were available to her. Most of the women in the community that were her age were married and had large families. This was not Berthina's intention. One child was enough for her. She still could remember what it felt like to be pregnant and big as a house; not to mention the pain of childbirth. But she did want a husband to take care of her both emotionally financially.

Jewel and Ward were quite busy making the social scenes in town. They could be seen at the "speak-easies" that were so popular. They were a great couple together. Each of them had learned to do the Charleston and could hardly wait for the weekend to come so they could go dancing. Because Jewel was so small he could swing her around the dance floor with ease. If there was a big crowd at the dances, they would be the entertainment of the evening. Jewel loved this attention and the nightlife that she and Ward were enjoying. It was a far cry from the drudgery at the gin or at home. While Berthina didn't give her consent to their activities, she was helpless to control her headstrong daughter. Jewel was nearly eighteen and certainly grown enough to make her own decisions. Partying in Greenwood and Carrollton soon became commonplace and they ventured to Indianola, and even to Jackson. Although it was a long way to Jackson, they frequently went there as a change of scenery and could dance the night away, returning to Greenwood in the wee hours of the morning. Jewel certainly realized this was a far cry from the type of life she had been having and she had to admit that it was fun.

Berthina did not have much interest in the gin. Jewel had been handling those affairs quite nicely, and Berthina made no demands to know the score there. She did have some information about the financial status when Jewel came to her insisting that they would need to sell some more of the farmland. Charlie Stanton had advised her to sell off a few hundred acres. Charlie felt they could get a good price for some of the land even though the whole country was in a depression and money was tight. Berthina knew that Charlie Stanton would not lead them astray and besides, she needed money to continue her search for a man. At this time Jewel did not hesitate to sell the land. She needed money to continue to run the gin and the household. However, it was not to be. Jewel had chosen a 200-

acre tract on the west side of the farm and instructed Charlie Stanton to procure a buyer for it. The day the transaction was to be final; Berthina and Jewel went to the Carrollton Bank to sign the papers. The banker explained to them the seriousness of the bank loans and the amount that was overdue on them. He calmly handed Berthina a check for $8.50 as the proceeds of the sale. She was bewildered and devastated. Surely the land Harvey left to her was more valuable than that! She always felt he had provided for her by owning farmland. However, she didn't understand the fact that the loans were long overdue. Regardless of what Jewel had been telling her, she just couldn't comprehend the fact that the bank came first when the land was sold. This confused Berthina since she felt the money should have been hers. The bank did not have that opinion and counseled her that she must pay the money on the notes or lose the entire farm. The gin was foundering for money to operate also. The larger cotton growers had found other means of ginning their cotton. The machinery at the Treadwell gin was outdated and constantly in need of repair. It was obvious to Jewel that the gin would soon be closed. She knew that there would not be enough money to continue running it much longer. This meant the farm would have to support all of them, which was doubtful.

 Jewel had been so busy taking in her own world that she had failed to notice that Berthina was practically out of her mourning stage. She was beginning to be seen at many of the events taking place in Carrollton and Greenwood. It had been nearly two years since Harvey was killed. The trial for Richard McLean was coming up and Berthina wondered what fate awaited him. Richard McLean had robbed her of her meal ticket and her future. She spoke often about going to the trial, which would be held in Greenwood at the County Court House. Jewel had no interest in being there. It was still too painful for her to witness the story again. She still had bad dreams about the whole sordid event and to relive it was not for Jewel. She preferred to push the whole mess to the back of her mind

Leflore County was a huge passel of land, stretching along the edge of the Florwood River. It was hilly and wooded. Timber would have been a good crop if hiding a moonshine still in the woods had not brought better returns. There was a sprinkling of small communities scattered around the hills and "hollers" as they were called by the local gentry. Stewartsville was just down the road "a piece" from Black Hawk. Coila was off to the north where a large academy for higher learning had been prior to the turn of the 20th century. Stanton, a very small town named for E.H.Stanton of Jackson, was on the main road to Carrollton. If you traveled to the southwest, you could go to Gravel Hill, which was as the name implied, a large knoll where the soil was mostly gravel. It was not tillable land and the farmers who lived there had to travel to someone else's farm to work. Most of the towns had only a general store or a church, which gave that community its identity. The towns were established during the horse and buggy days when very few food items were bought. Some housewives bought staples such as flour or sugar from the local stores. Many of them bought their necessary items from the peddlers that still ran the routes from house to house. Nearly everything else was "home grown". Most people in the communities raised a sizeable garden and the housewife was expected to "can" the produce for their winter meals. The stores stocked feed for livestock or repair parts for wagons as well as lamp chimneys and coal oil.

The county seat of Leflore County was Greenwood, which lay to the west and north of the Black Hawk community. The County courthouse was a big ominous building situated in the middle of a square. The streets all came together at the Court Square. There were shade trees and benches where the locals could seat themselves and watch the world go by. Many of the older generation would come to town daily and simply sit around the courthouse all day. These men were unable to work as hard in the fields as their offspring and this was their way to get through the day. This was the method of passing the news around from town to town. It was also the gossip gin of the community. If you went to Greenwood on business, it was an all day event. The whole family traveled with a picnic lunch complete with lemonade to be enjoyed under the shade of a tree on the courthouse lawn. If you were fortunate enough to own a car, the procedure was much the same with the exception of the travel time, which was cut by about an hour. Families rarely went to Greenwood to run errands. If you made the trip it was an excursion.

Law-less-ness was the law in Leflore County. Murders went unpunished if you could find the prosecutor, and pay him a month's salary in advance to look the other way. The sheriff and judge were often on the take and consistently turned their head at crimes of passion or a dispute over moonshine running boundaries. Attempts to clean up the county by law-abiding citizens had been thwarted many times when a complaining citizen was simply eliminated in an "unfortunate accident". It was always very difficult to find an eyewitness or someone willing to testify to the wrong deed. Because the local citizenry lived in fear of reprisals, they continued to live their lives as circumspectly as possible and avoided any confrontations with the law. One such incident that left the locals pondering the sad state of affairs happened at a Sunday school picnic. Two Sunday school classes were having a friendly game of softball. It was a hot summer day and there were many families in attendance at the ballgame. There had been "dinner on the ground" as it was referred to when the entire church congregation came together for a picnic. Wagons were put together to serve as tables for the spread of food and folks simply filled a plate and ate their lunch on a blanket spread on the ground. On this beautiful Sunday afternoon the softball game had been in full swing and it was the feature entertainment of the day. The song leader of the church was on the pitcher's mound when the batter disputed his ability to pitch properly. Suddenly the batter charged to confront the pitcher in anger. An argument came to a disastrous end when the batter swung his bat, hitting the pitcher in the head, killing him instantly. A prominent family was left in mourning and the community was in shock at such a dastardly deed. The talk of the community was centered mostly about the punishment that would be meted out to the killer. Because there were so many witnesses to the event, there was hardly any question of his guilt. Things were about to take a strange turn. Rumor was that the defendant intended to plead "self-defense" which would bring a question to anyone's mind about just how he felt he needed to defend himself. On the day of the trial, held in Greenwood, the courtroom was packed long before the time of the trial. The defense attorney was a member of the church and of the softball team. Apparently he did not have a very good sense of right and wrong. He arrived at the courthouse before trial time and set the clock ahead one hour. When the judge arrived, he noted the hour and asked about the defendant. The attorney simply stated that his client was a little late. Not realizing the deception, the judge sentenced him to one year in jail "in absentia". The entire county was shocked by such a miscarriage of justice but felt there was little they could do. It would be years before anyone attempted to "clean-up" Leflore County. That effort would ultimately exact a mighty price from the family of Blandon Planer, a newly elected lawman.

The murder of Harvey Treadwell was simply another case in point of the ineffectiveness of the court system. Harvey had owned a lot of land in Leflore County. He was a hard-nosed, no nonsense, businessman who ran his business his way. He had little sympathy for slackers. He was particularly critical of men whom he felt did not support their families. He allowed farmers in the area to rent his farms. But Harvey expected the ultimate from his land tenants. If the farmer worked hard, he could raise enough to feed his family for the winter, but rarely earned enough to live beyond abject poverty. If Harvey felt the farmer was not working hard enough, he would take the land back, and lend it to someone else the following year.

Such was the case of Richard McLean. He was a hot tempered "country boy" who had grown up below the poverty line. He had been the oldest of 11 children and had spent most of his working days supporting the younger kids. His father was a bootlegger of renown and was constantly on the run from someone. The other bootleggers resented his success in the "illegal pursuit of his fortune". And the revenuers were constantly on his trail. Richard had seen his father shot and near death on several occasions only to watch him recover and return to his ill gotten gains. The family faced near starvation most of the time. Because of the danger the family seemed to always be facing, Richard carried a pistol in his boot. He made no effort to conceal it and dismissed any queries about it by saying it was for his own protection. When Harvey Treadwell agreed to let Richard farm some of his land for a 50/50 share it was like a miracle to him. He was concerned his only other option would be to follow in his father's footsteps. He farmed a part of Harvey's land but not to Harvey's satisfaction. Harvey considered him lazy and constantly taunted him about his work habits. Harvey probably had some dislike for the man because of the reputation of his father; however, he had a plot of ground that could be profitable for both of them if Richard worked it. Richard's wife had been ill for quite some time. In the last year she had been bedridden with tuberculosis and was gravely ill. They had a child and Richard was trying to nurse his wife to better health and take care of his child at the same time. Working his farmland was becoming increasingly difficult. The more Harvey provoked him the more Richard stewed about his unfortunate predicament. And, to add insult to injury, Richard had difficulty controlling his hot temper. Needless to say all of these ingredients formed a boiling pot of resentment between the two men. Richard decided he had a good crop of cotton and it would bring him enough cash to make it through the winter months. He brought it to the gin but he kept a watchful eye on Harvey. He was convinced that Harvey would cheat him. Many of his fellow farmers knew of the disputes between them and had goaded Richard into a near frenzy over the treatment Harvey meted out to them as well as to him. When the cotton was cut and ready for market, Harvey paid Richard what he felt he was due, however, Richard felt otherwise. He argued with him but soon realized it was a useless cause. Harvey stood his ground, dismissing Richard in an offhand manner. Richard walked away, but as the story goes, he called Harvey out to the doorway of the gin. When Harvey appeared, and in plain view of the other workers at the gin he pulled his pistol from his boot and shot him.

The trial for Richard McLean began in the spring of 1931. The days were still cool so the temperature inside the courthouse was still bearable. McLean was well known in the Black Hawk community, but not so popular in Greenwood. However, he had a local following. He had been released on bail of $10 since the day after the shooting. He continued to live on the farm that he had rented from Harvey Treadwell. He attempted to work the farm as a means of income. His wife had died of tuberculosis, shortly after the murder, and he lived with his daughter in the house. He made every effort to provide a home for her and raise the child as best he could without the help of his deceased wife. Although there were many available women in his community and most of them willing to assume the role of mothering the child, he had chosen not to pursue a stepmother for his daughter. He was sure he would be sent away to prison, and he couldn't imagine leaving his daughter with someone whom he had only known a short time. His parents had agreed to take the child if Richard was sent to prison. While he knew she would just be mixed in with the other children in the household, and subjected to the same brand of lifestyle he had overcome, he felt he really had no other choice.

The day of the trial was peppered with thunderstorms adding an ominous air to the pending case. With every bolt of lightning or clap of thunder, the atmosphere in the courtroom became so electrically charged that the trial became a suspense thriller even before it began. The visitor's gallery was filled with citizens from Black Hawk and neighboring Carrollton. Everyone wondered what would happen to Richard. The crowd was astir with the excitement of the trial. At the same time, Harvey Treadwell had been a prominent citizen, well respected in the community. Everyone seemed to know that his daughter, Jewel, had taken over the business and was acting as though she was Harvey Treadwell, incarnate. Harvey had been generous with his money, but he also was very difficult to get along with, so the crowd was split about 50/50. Some felt that Harvey deserved what he got because he had been mistreating the tenants on his land for a long time. Others were sympathetic with Harvey in that he had given them money when they needed it until they could bring in the next crop. And even those who knew the next crop would never come in, they still had an allegiance to Harvey.

The judge entered the courtroom and the bailiff asked the gallery to rise in respect for "His Honor". The judge then asked the defendant to rise and state his name for all to hear. He asked for the plea from Richard McLean, to which Richard replied that he was not guilty. No one in the courtroom expected this plea from a man who had admitted to everyone that he pulled the trigger. He seemed adamant in his plea that he should not be considered guilty of the murder of Harvey Treadwell. His attorney stood silently by while the prosecutor expounded upon the case before him. The prosecutor pointed out to the court that Richard McLean had called Harvey to the doorway where he could get a clear shot. He also stated that Richard had been so callused in his deed that he nonchalantly went to the Stewart home to clean up. He pointed out to the judge that Richard had long had a feud with Harvey Treadwell and he had planned this murder for quite some time.

Richard McLean was called to the stand. The defense attorney asked him to state what happened on December 5, 1930. Richard calmly stated that Harvey Treadwell had cheated him out of a fair price for his cotton. He also stated that he thought this had happened to others and that the talk around Black Hawk was that someone should speak up about the treatment they had been receiving at the hands of Harvey Treadwell. Richard stated that he thought it was time to be heard, and he was just the one to do it. The judge then asked Richard about his personal life, inquiring of his daughter and his plans for her future. When Richard had completed telling the story of his wife's tragic death and his attempt to provide shelter and education for the child, the judge raised his gavel, struck it one time on the table and sentenced the culprit to one year in the county jail.

Case closed!

Berthina Treadwell rose to leave the courtroom and could hardly believe her ears. She knew very little about any kind of legal trials or courtroom procedure and she knew she had no control over this event. She calmly left the building and returned to her home in Greenwood.

There was some talk in the community about a miscarriage of justice. But there were those who took a serious lesson from this experience. The punishment for murder in Leflore County was so slight; many of the local gentry sometimes felt it was worth it.

Life in Leflore County went on as usual. Some spoke of the lesson to be learned from this event was; human life was so cheap in Leflore County that many more lives would be lost before the local gentry would rise up against the lack of justice.

CHAPTER NINE

The Marriage

Jewel and Ward had continued to see each other as often as they could. Their partying continued and they had become the talk of the community. Jewel had worried about what was happening to her and the questions would occupy her every waking moment and certainly the greatest of these was her future with Ward.

They continued to attend the Mt. Pleasant Christian Church on a regular basis, and could be seen at most of the functions at the church, however, they seemed to be straying from her basic beliefs. Social life in Black Hawk was limited to the events at the church or an occasional party at someone's home. "Taffy pulls" where a group of young people gathered together and made candy were a common event in the winter. Ice cream socials on the church lawn were the summer feature. Jewel and Ward took part in all the activities in and around the church but seemed to prefer the rowdier life style they found in and around Leflore County as well as venturing into Jackson to party with friends. Berthina had ceased to complain about Jewel's behavior and her association with Ward because she was busy being an attractive and eligible widow. Jewel continued to be an avid Bible student and became well versed in the Bible even though her behavior was a bit outside of religious circles. When she thought about her association with Ward, she remembered a Bible verse found in Joel 2:25. It stated that the Lord would restore the years the locusts had eaten. She felt this meant that she could have a renewed life of her own beyond the tragedies of her father and the fire.

The farm was almost all sold off or forfeited to the bank. Some of it had been sold to individual farmers but each time there was a sale, the majority of the money went to the bank for the unpaid notes and mortgages. Charlie Stanton had attempted to convince Berthina she should sell the land, but when she tried to sell it the Bank took the money. Jewel had made several attempts to sell the timber, but the Depression was so severe in Leflore County, there was no market for the timber. Most of the farmers who had been on a 50/50 basis with Harvey could no longer afford to continue to buy seed or hire the help to plant their crops. Some of them found other people in the county with whom they could farm with a better split but for the most part, farming the Treadwell farm was over. The only land left was about 400 acres and it was mostly timber.

Jewel was not happy to see the farm go. She felt betrayed by her mother in that she had made very little effort to keep the farm. And she couldn't "get her arms around" the fact that Berthina didn't know HOW to save her inheritance. Jewel knew there was very little money, but she still had held the hope that somehow they could save the property. It seemed that everyone was losing their land. The bank was foreclosing on a lot of their neighbors and for a while it seemed the bank owned more of Leflore County than the people did.

Jewel had other interests on her mind. The gin was closed and the farm was gone. Occupying her mind was something totally different. She and Ward were very much in love and she was busy making a life of her own. There was precious little money coming in and Jewel wasn't sure how she should earn a living. She had no association with her mother and she felt she had no one to turn to except Ward and by this time he was working for his father in the auto repair business. He had a steady income and Jewel had nothing. She looked upon Ward as a ticket to somewhere, she just wasn't sure where. While her mother was busy in her own search for a husband, one rainy night in March, Jewel and Ward quietly slipped across the Florwood River to Indianola, and were married. They were excited newly-weds. For a wedding present, they asked Berthina for 200 acres of land for themselves. Berthina complained bitterly, but obliged them and deeded them the last parcel of land that had been owned by Harvey Treadwell. They had little or no money when they married, so they promptly sold the land and took off to New Orleans on a honeymoon. This one action was totally against what Jewel believed about selling the land, but she was desperate for money and she was in love. Life was carefree and good. They had Harvey's truck and Ward could keep it in good repair. They felt they were living the high life. No one told them the old adage about "the higher the flight, the harder the fall".

CHAPTER TEN

The Newlyweds

It was a time when the entire country was in The Big Depression, and the dreams of high society of Ward and Jewel were soon shattered when they had spent all of their money. While Jewel had a good head on her shoulders for business, she was a lot like other young people of her day. They still had their emotions. Sometimes their ideas are shortsighted. Reality soon set in on the newly weds of 1932. They returned to Greenwood and set up housekeeping in a small house that they shared with Berthina. If Jewel thought she was getting away from Berthina when she married, she had to think again. Berthina had no place to go and no income so they all shared a house together. Ward went back to work for his father and Jewel remained at home trying to establish a life for them. However, Jewel was ill equipped to be a housewife. Berthina was not much better and refused to help in any way. Jewel had lived in a home where hired help was a given. She knew nothing about how to cook, clean house or make a home. Most women that she knew could sew. They made their own curtains or their own clothes. Many of their friends grew a large garden and the housewife "canned" the vegetables for the winter meals. While Ward grew the garden, neither Berthina nor Jewel knew how to preserve anything that could be used in the winter. The apples that grew in the yard were eaten as they ripened. Jewel remembered when Nedra had taken much of the apple and pear crop to the "root cellar" that was on the old home place and kept them until they were made into pies in the winter. Jewel had no idea how to bake a pie or "can" the tomatoes that Ward had grown in the garden. She didn't choose to follow any of the plans for survival that she had watched Nedra do. There had always been hired help to do those things and now that was a thing of the past for her. She wondered if she should have learned those things when she watched Nedra in the kitchen. Suddenly at the age of 18 she was forced to become domesticated. She struggled with the daily chores of cooking and cleaning. And she didn't really want to do these things. Jewel had never tasted poverty as it was currently thrust upon her. In her frustration, she turned to her first love; reading and studying the Bible. Life was rather dull in Greenwood and there was no money to spend on anything beyond rent and groceries. The only pleasure trip they allowed themselves was their Sunday trip to church at Black Hawk. It seemed their partying days were gone and with it came boredom. Jewel and Ward continued their life together enjoying each other as best they could in a world they were ill equipped to handle. Their social life had become centered around the church and little else. In the early spring of 1934, Jewel discovered she was pregnant. While she was not overjoyed at the thought, it was sure to provide a diversion in an otherwise humdrum life.

CHAPTER ELEVEN

Belinda & Yvonne

Jewel's pregnancy was rather uneventful even though it was a new experience for her. She had known other young women who had endured the event with more enthusiasm than Jewel could muster. Her mother had warned her about "morning sickness" but nothing anyone had described equaled the actual curse. Each morning as Ward was leaving for work, she could hardly get to her feet before she would be hanging over the basin leaving her daily deposit even before she had a chance to eat anything. She wondered how life could get any worse. Jewel was such a tiny woman and when she had gained twenty-five pound she felt like a rhinoceros. She later commented that those nine months seemed like a lifetime to her.

Belinda Frederickson was born on February 5, 1935 to Jewel Treadwell Frederickson and Randall Ward Frederickson. She weighed almost eight pounds and came into the world after only a few hours of labor. She was a pretty baby with hair tinted the color of the fall leaves. She didn't appear to be a newborn baby as her skin was milky white. It appeared that her eyes would be green just like her mother's. She was healthy and active from the very beginning. She favored her grandmother, Berthina, and seemed to be restless from the start. She seemed discontent with Jewel's attempt at nursing her and finally became a bottle baby. Jewel didn't object to that since she disliked the idea of baring her breast for any reason. Jewel made every effort to be a good mother and she spent hours playing with her new baby. She read to her and tried to settle her restless spirit. Belinda had a mind of her own and was very hard to control. As she grew into her childhood, her personality never changed and later in life, she would show signs of her early years as they manifested themselves in her adult life.

Ward showed little fatherly interest in the baby and avoided the responsibilities of fatherhood, preferring instead to sashay around Greenwood with his friends. He was a dapper man, who dressed in the latest fashion and was considered to be quite a gentleman. He had a great knack for working on cars, but he changed from his greasy clothes into his "Sunday" clothes as soon as possible after work hours. He never wanted to appear to be a "commoner". He was not an educated man and he did not have the mind that Jewel had. Ward would rather play cards with friends than be caught reading a book. Babies were not his "thing" and because Jewel always seemed to be in control, he was almost totally eliminated from the household until after the baby was bedded down for the night. If he was at home, they would play cards or listen to the radio. Often as not he would be late getting home, long after Jewel had gone to bed. Her stamina had been tireless when she was working at the farm or gin, but being a housewife seemed to sap her strength. Many nights she would be in bed asleep when Ward came home. So their time spent together was very limited.

Jewel was not endowed with the gift of motherhood. She loved her baby very much but she still preferred to be on the farm. The farm was long gone. The gin was gone. Jewel made sure the baby was cared for although she had a difficult time handling a baby, and the household chores. The household never seemed to be in order no matter how hard Jewel tried. Belinda was barely a year old, walking and trying to talk when Jewel discovered she was pregnant again. This fact so infuriated her that she railed against Ward as if he had created this situation all on his own. Some days she wondered where the glory days of her single life had gone. She didn't wear her pregnancy well and was beset with morning sickness again for the entire nine months. The task of caring for Belinda, handling the events of the household and being pregnant made Jewel an almost unbearable person to come home to. She continually assured Ward that this would be her last baby by whatever means it took. Ward did not take that announcement lightly. He could still remember the days of their courtship and wondered what had happened to them. He had a hard time blaming himself for the lack of love in the household. He was convinced that he had not changed. There was no money to continue their partying days but even their time together in the evenings was strained and uncomfortable.

Jewel survived the summer of 1936 as a cumbersome pregnant mother. It was hot and humid like every other summer had been, but this year was a "worse than the others" type of season and she barely survived it, both mentally and physically. When Yvonne was born on September 19, 1936 she was a delight to her mother. She seemed to resemble her grandfather, Harvey, and maybe Jewel was mellowing. No matter the reason, Jewel looked upon the tiny form as a wonder to behold. Yvonne, as she was soon called, had coal black hair and fair complexion. If Belinda was a problem child, Yvonne made up for it in her docility. She was a good-natured baby and required only the bare minimum of care. She slept and ate on a regular basis and aside from the usual feeding and changing of diapers tended to be maintenance free. Maybe God has a sense of humor after all, because if Yvonne had been otherwise, the question remains of how Jewel could have handled the situation.

Things were not good at the Frederickson home. Ward was excluded from most of the daily activities with the girls and Jewel's interest in him had waned as well. To further complicate matters, Berthina meddled in their daily affairs regularly. She continued to berate him for all his failures and faults and seemed to overlook the fact that he worked daily and provided his family with a place to live and food to eat. Even though Berthina had married and left the Frederickson family behind, she continued to offer her opinion on their lifestyle. Ward's interest in cars had continued to grow and he worked daily in his father's garage in Greenwood. Many of the townspeople now owned an automobile and, because of the infancy of the industry, cars required regular maintenance. Most people who owned a car had little or no knowledge of repairing one. Some of the farmers had a little knowledge of repairing a car unless it was a transmission problem. Tractors did not have transmissions therefore a car would present a different problem. The ability to afford a car also allowed the owner the ability to pay someone for service to it. The Frederickson Garage did a good business and Ward was able to provide for Jewel and the girls - even if his presence at home was in question.

Jewel was not a happy person at this time in her life. She ruled the household and Ward with an iron hand. Her demands on him were almost without measure. She seemed to wake each morning in a bad mood and continue through the day the same way. Conversations with Ward were accusatory and demeaning. Her attitude about life in general was surly. She demanded his money but gave nothing of herself in return. She insisted on having hired help although very few young families could afford such a luxury. After all, she was Harvey Treadwell's daughter and she had never known domesticity. And she didn't want to learn now.

By 1938 Ward Frederickson was beginning to see the uselessness of his marriage. If he ever thought he could live with Jewel in harmony, every new day proved him wrong. His dream of sharing her money, her life, his children, or a return to the good old days had become his worst nightmare. The farm was gone, the gin was gone and the love they shared in their moments of passion was gone as well. Jewel was demanding all he could make at the garage. If Ward had been busy haunting the old lifestyle with other women, it was never told. But, it was certain that life at home was barren for him. He surmised that he was still a young man of 26 and surely deserved some happiness of his own. It appeared that it would have to happen without Jewel. He hardly knew his daughters and he felt he would have to support them, but he felt he could live without their mother.

While Ward was contemplating his next move, Jewel was in her car traveling to Jackson to see Charlie Stanton. The story she told him concerning Ward was somewhat different, if not untrue, from what he might have heard from Ward. Regardless of who did what to whom, Jewel Frederickson wanted a divorce. She wanted Ward to support the girls with everything but his life's blood. She also wanted the house and all their worldly possessions. Ward was one jump ahead of Jewel this time. He had already been to a lawyer in Greenwood and made his move to divorce her first. He was not going to live the life of celibacy and that's what she was offering him. Plus, the chaos at home was almost unbearable. He sought his divorce in the Leflore County court system. His memory served him well and it told him that any legal judgments in Leflore County grossly leaned in favor of anyone that chose to buck a Treadwell. No doubt he felt this was his first stroke of good luck in a, so far, luckless life with Jewel Treadwell Fredrickson.

Their divorce became final in 1938 and Jewel moved to Jackson with the girls. Ward paid his support to the girls and rarely saw them. The animosity between Ward and Jewel was so thick you could almost cut it with a knife. Whatever the outcome, Ward knew that he was the winner no matter what, since he no longer had to deal with Jewel or her mother. He wondered every day how he could be so lucky. Ward Frederickson went on to establish a good life of his own without the baggage of a Treadwell. He remarried in 1939 and fathered a daughter. She would become a half sister to Belinda and Yvonne, but never had any association with either of them.

CHAPTER TWELVE

Jewel Gets a Step-Father

Berthina Treadwell had little or no money, having lost it all during the Depression. Harvey had left quite a fortune, but it was all "on paper". Berthina had never had to deal with the financial matters and Jewel had been helpless to save the inheritance her father had left to them. Berthina's only child had virtually washed her hands of her mother. They had never been on good terms, and Jewel grew weary of Berthina's complaining. Managing the farm problems was out of the capabilities of Berthina and she raped the proceeds from any sales of the farmland, if she could wrench it away from the bank. She squandered it all on material things for herself. Her opinion was that she needed to look as good as possible and live as high as possible to snag another man to take care of her.

She spent the first two years of her widowhood looking around every corner for a prospective husband. Most of the people in Greenwood knew her and understood her motives. However, she was still a stunning woman. She had kept her girlish figure and spent time and money accenting her assets as best she could. She knew there was someone out there for her somewhere. She was more interested in finding someone for material reasons than to satisfy any affairs of the heart.

In 1932, Berthina had been living in Greenwood with Jewel and Ward. The rule that no two women can live in the same house could have easily been written about Jewel and Berthina. They had never been friends and now they were under the same roof. Berthina considered Jewel her little girl and treated her that way. Jewel was more grown up than most women twice her age and she gave her mother this information on a daily basis as if it were a dose of vitamins. Life at the Frederickson home was constant chaos. Regardless of the situation Berthina had no other place to live. She was forced to endure the set up no matter whether she liked it or not.

In the spring of 1933, she met Dr. James Franke, a veterinarian from Yazoo City, a town about thirty miles to the southwest. He had previously been married and had two daughters. He was a recent widower and had known Berthina for many years. He had known Harvey and knew that he ran his business with an iron hand. He had sympathy for Berthina and felt he could solve her problem of loneliness. She was certainly a lovely lady and he felt comfortable squiring her around the communities to any event. He thought he could win her heart and that she would make him a good wife. If Berthina felt the same about him, it was a surprise to everyone who knew them. Berthina hated the life she was living with Jewel and Ward and his marriage proposal sounded like a breath of fresh air

– or maybe an escape route. Nevertheless, Berthina and Dr. Franke were married that year and she moved into his house in Yazoo City. Berthina set out to make it her home and did her best to fit into Dr. Franke's world. He had money and she spent it. They were active in the society of Greenwood, Yazoo City, and Jackson, making the rounds of garden parties, teas, and church affairs. Their activities in the night-life of all the communities was legendary. They never missed a party or formal ball. Because of his medical profession, he was invited to every social event for miles around. Berthina loved this lifestyle albeit, short lived. The marriage was off to a rocky start. Dr. Franke had a serious drinking problem. Apparently everyone knew about his drinking except Berthina. She may have known about this terrible habit and maybe she chose not to see it. If she thought she could cure him of this vice, she found she was up against a stone wall.

In a short time after she married Dr. Franke, Berthina discovered she was pregnant. The very thought of childbirth made her cringe in pain. She could still remember the birth of Jewel, and she wanted no part of that scene again. Berthina did not want another child to care for, however she was there and it was to be. She took her wrath out on Dr. Franke and he handled it with grace, fortitude, and a flask in his hip pocket. He wasn't pleased at her reaction to such a glorious event. He looked forward to the impending birth of _his_ child. Since Berthina was so cantankerous he was forced to lose himself in the bottle even more, drinking himself into oblivion almost daily.

Percy Bradford Franke was born in the spring of 1934. Berthina survived this birth much as she had her first child. She was proud of her new son and instantly had a surge of motherly feelings. However, it was short lived. She knew that once again she would need to lose this paunchy look and regain her former figure. Dr. Franke was delighted that he had fathered a son. He proudly broadcast the news far and wide. Jewel nature. Berthina loved the attention that her husband gave her but there was no method of birth control in 1934 and she was traumatized at the thought of being pregnant again. She had witnessed many of her friends who seemed to have one baby after another. She had no intention of living like that. If she refused to make love to her husband, he would simply have to accept life that way. And, she had no patience with his drinking habit, which he seemed helpless to curtail. No amount of bribery or cajoling from Berthina had any effect on Dr. Franke's love for the hard stuff. All these circumstances together made life almost unbearable at the Franke home. Partying and playing away from home was the only way they could live together. Dr. Franke had a mean streak, particularly when he had been drinking. On more than one occasion, Berthina would be sporting a blackened eye or a large bruise would be evident on her face. She made some excuse about the evidence of his abuse and attempted to hide her devastation that she was an abused wife. His physical abuse during drunken bouts was never discussed, but his verbal abuse was constant and in public. If Berthina was able to hide the constant physical abuse, the public ridicule by her husband was more than she could take. Berthina weighed her options and determined she had never known an alcoholic, had never been abused, and she didn't plan to continue living this way. Berthina rarely asked Jewel's opinion about any decision she needed to make, but this time she sought Jewel's judgment on this event. Even though they had little in common, Berthina needed Jewel's consent for her own peace of mind. Early one morning in June of 1936, Berthina arrived at the back door of Jewel's house, clutching the hand of Percy with one hand, and holding her bandaged arm up to shield her black and blue face. Her right eye was nearly swollen shut. She was hysterically screaming and seemed incoherent. It seems that Dr. Franke had wreaked havoc on Berthina because of her constant complaining about his drinking habits. He proceeded to beat Berthina with a club he kept by the back door to correct the dog. When she had tried to shield Percy from this onslaught, he proceeded to be even more vicious, screaming many obscenities at her. Jewel stared in horror at her mother, and, for the first time that Jewel could remember, the two women embraced and cried, inconsolably, together. The sight of her mother in this condition touched a nerve in Jewel that she could hardly comprehend. Although she and her mother had never been close, this was far too devastating to believe. Jewel was appalled at the brutality she was witnessing and the thought crossed her mind that she, herself, could kill him if she had a chance. The two women quietly went to see old Doc Rogers, who was in his late 80's, for consultation. He set Berthina's broken arm and bandaged her cuts, and showed her how to apply an ice pack to her bruises. He also promised anonymity to both of them. Jewel quickly gave her blessing to a divorce from this evil man even though it was against her Christian principles.

After only three years of marriage, Berthina sued Dr. Franke for a divorce. The physical abuse was never mentioned, however, it was hardly a secret in the community. All of the Treadwell clan rallied around Berthina and supported her during the tough times while the divorce was pending. They had never been sympathetic to Berthina in the past but this time they felt she was justified in her actions. Dr. Franke was not very well liked by the family and most of them felt that Berthina could find someone who would be good to her and help take care of Percy.

The marriage of Berthina and Dr. Franke ended in the summer of 1936, and she managed to get support from him that would take care of Percy. Berthina was a young woman and she felt she would be able to find someone else, once the trauma of the divorce was behind her. The divorce action really affected her. Not many women would seek a divorce in the 30's. It was just not an acceptable procedure. Women were expected to stay with their husbands no matter what happened in the marriage. Unfortunately the future held a similar experience for Jewel in the not too distant months.

Berthina did not wear her single status well. She had not liked being a widow and now her life as a divorcee left her even more depressed. Her experience with Dr. Franke had shattered her completely. She had expected to feel that being single was better than being married to him. What she experienced was that most of the friends they had as a couple were not interested in including her as a divorcee'. While she had enjoyed the social life, the fact that their parties always ended in a drunken brawl where she was the object of his tirades left a lasting impression on her. Berthina was a docile person and hated the confrontations she was forced to endure with him. Now she simply wanted to get on with her life. And it appeared that she would have to make new friends or be a hermit. She longed for the former not the latter.

Although she had just been granted a divorce, she still longed for someone in her life. She seemed tireless in her search for someone to take care of her. She not only needed financial support, but she needed emotional support. Needless to say, many men were available and she commanded a lot of attention no matter where she went. She was still a beautiful woman and her impeccable wardrobe was always the latest in fashion. The primary problem that bedeviled her was that her motives were so obvious to everyone. Most men found her to be forbidden fruit. Berthina decided that she needed new territory. She moved to Jackson, no doubt, thinking the field of eligible men would be larger. And most of the new prospects did not know about her past as a divorcee' or a widow. Even though she wanted a man on her arm, she longed for female companionship as well. If she had women friends she felt she could be at ease in the social scene as a single person.

Because she and Jewel were not on the best of terms, she had to find someplace to live on her own. And, Jewel had one daughter and was about to give birth to her second baby. Berthina and Percy were forced to make a way for themselves. Of course, she had managed to get a sizeable amount of support from Dr. Franke by convincing him that he would want the best for his son. Life in Jackson promised to be good and she had substantial means to travel in all the best circles in her search for a new life.

Berthina needed some means of support and wanted to contribute to her own income. She quickly was hired at a department store in Jackson. She began as sales clerk selling ladies lingerie. She was a fashionable lady so she was able to demonstrate what a well-dressed southern belle would need to wear. And this type of employment offered her the opportunity to display her own talent in assisting the ladies who were shopping for the finer things for themselves. It was a far cry from the dowdy women she had known in Leflore county whom she felt were content with the muslin drawers they made at home for themselves out of the feed sacks that had once housed the chickens' feed. She was convinced that women wanted the nice "undies" but were unsure of just how to purchase them for their own personal use. Berthina was right at home in this atmosphere. In just a short time, the manager of the store saw the potential in Berthina and quickly made her the department manager. Before long she took over the management of the entire second floor of the store and was handling about a dozen sales girls in all of the ladies "ready to wear" departments. It was the first time in her adult life that Berthina felt useful and it was probably her happiest days.

Shortly after she came to Jackson, Berthina was back in the dating scene. She joined every organization she could and became a typical "Southern Belle". Most of the women in her circle of friends were married and they were wary of this lovely but lonely woman whom their husbands might find attractive. Berthina had a difficult time finding eligible men in these circles so her next plan of action was to find a church that might have a recent widower in attendance. She joined Salem Christian Church to peruse the membership for a new candidate. She really wanted the social life, but not necessarily the life of a wife. Her wishes were soon to come true. She was squired around the circles of high society by a number of men from the church. Since there were many church parties, she was given the chance to enjoy the life she favored. She was cautious not to alienate any of her married friends. She needed them to arrange for someone to take her to the church functions. She was also very cognizant of the position she was in when it came to her being overly friendly with their husbands. She guarded her self so as not to appear a flirt. Even though she had a small child at home, Dr. Franke had provided for a nanny to care for Percy, giving her the freedom to pursue her lifestyle. While she now was a grandmother to two girls, Berthina did not spend much time being a "nanna" to either of them. She was busy socializing and enjoying every minute of it.

In the fall of 1939 Berthina met a man named Willard Rainey. He was originally from a small town called Ada but had recently moved to Jackson. He worked for the Liberty Barrel, a company, as the name implies, which made storage barrels. He was smitten by the charms of Berthina just like the others before him had been. He was a recent widower and felt his loneliness too. If he was searching for a wife, he didn't show it. He fell head over heels in love with this beautiful divorcee' and it appeared that she felt the same. He apparently didn't see her shallowness, or maybe he chose to overlook it. During the winter of 1939 they could be seen at nearly every social gathering in Jackson. They were certainly enjoying each other. After only a short courtship he asked her to marry him. Needless to say, Berthina agreed. Mr. Rainey was older than Berthina so she felt sure he would not expect her to have more children. Berthina was now 50 years old, but looked more like 40. Percy was 5 years old, and she was certain her childbearing years were behind her. She and Mr. Rainey could enjoy life to the fullest without any concerns about children. After all, this grandmother could not be expected to continue to propagate. Jewel was not against the marriage since she had problems of her own to deal with and could hardly take on the affairs of her mother. Berthina had long been headstrong but naïve about the future problems any marriage brings. Jewel knew the best thing to do was just let her mother do whatever she wanted and allow her to suffer her own consequences. Besides, Jewel had a life of her own and was struggling with her own identity. The promise she had made to her father as he lay dying haunted her every day.

Berthina slipped right into the new marriage with ease. Mr. Rainey loved his new stepson and Dr. Franke was pleased that Percy had a male image in the home to influence him. For the first time since Harvey had been killed, Berthina appeared to have real feelings for Mr. Rainey. He was attentive and affectionate; two traits that Berthina had longed for since becoming a widow. Since there was no fear of future pregnancies, Berthina had a freedom to express herself that perhaps she had never had. She had always longed to be loved and now it seemed to be the right time. Mr. & Mrs. Rainey settled into the good life in Jackson.

CHAPTER THIRTEEN

Jackson & J.R.

After her divorce from Ward, Jewel and the two girls had moved to Jackson. She really wanted to get away from Greenwood and the memories that seemed to haunt her. She wanted to renew her spiritual life. She felt she had strayed from her faith in the last five years, and now it was time to repent and start over. She joined Salem Christian Church where her mother was attending. Although they attended the same church, they did not move in the same circles. Jewel was resigned to being a single mother. She did not actively seek companionship. She felt she needed to concentrate on being the best mother possible to her daughters. She wanted them to be in the church surroundings and she knew they needed a good education. Ward was supporting them the best he could with the money he made from his father's garage. Jewel had hired a nanny to help with the girls while she tried to find a job. She had no education, having left school at sixteen when her father was killed, and so her chances of finding a job were not good. She was quite astute at doing secretarial work or handling financial work for any company, but she could not afford to hire the nanny to stay with the girls full time. For the first time in her life Jewel felt stymied by her inability to rise above her status. She had little opportunity to have a social life. She had no extra cash and she found herself preoccupied with the girls. Jewel could remember when she enjoyed the partying with Ward, but now she seemed content to be a good mother. She occasionally would attend parties at the church but somehow felt out of sync. One evening she went to a party with a girl friend. It was an evening in October 1939, and the party was held at the Hanson Hotel. It was a grand and glorious party heralding in the fall season. Jewel had rustled up her best party dress and agreed to attend this event. She did not have the idea that she might find a mate at the party. She simply thought of it as a chance to go somewhere. She did not know who would be there but was assured that there would be many eligible men at the party. Many of her friends thought it was important for Jewel to meet some eligible men. She was not impressed. However, as luck would have it she met a man named J.R. Matthews.

J.R. Matthews was an entrepreneur of the first rank. In the early part of the 1930's he had several businesses, but unfortunately the Depression had all but wiped him out of business. He was not alone in this position as most of the businesses in the country failed at that time. Some of the wealthiest men in business failed to survive the hard times of the early 30s. He had taken it in his stride and immediately made other attempts to pull himself up by his own bootstraps. He was not one to be penniless for very long.

His creativity and business sense propelled him into new ventures. He was a great marketer and salesman. He could envision ways to make money faster than a racehorse could run. He had many contacts in the Jackson area and most of them knew he would be back on top again soon. He knew how to develop a business plan and he was always able to find financial backers for his ideas. By the late 1930's J.R. developed a company called the "Dumbling Toy Company." Maybe he thought it would be a dumb idea but hoped for its success. Regardless of his doubts or expectations, the Dumbling Toys were a huge success. "The Dumble Buggy", one of J.R.'s creations, made him a millionaire. The vehicle type of toy was an instant success because of its popularity with parents of every four-year-old. It was manufactured on a steel frame that could be propelled with their feet pushing themselves and creating a type of moving car. A child could become an instant driver and honk the horn on the steering wheel, just like dad, without leaving his living room. It was a safe toy for children since the body of the car was cast of seamless plastic – a new type of material for the 40's. The frame was tubular steel that meant it would not tip over and it was durable enough to withstand the most aggressive "driver". The cost was small making it available for nearly every child.

J.R.'s company manufactured a great number of other toys. He was flying high when he agreed to go to the party at the Hanson Hotel. His financial success was assured and his "pockets were lined with gold". J.R. had never heard of Jewel Frederickson but certainly did a double take when he saw her. Jewel was still a sight to behold. She was petite, redheaded, and feisty. She was smart even without an education but knew enough to not show her lack of schooling. She was a lady in every sense of the word and had a bit of a style that made her the envy of all the women around her. She gained the attention of all the men at the party without even trying.

J.R. was introduced to her and he couldn't get her out of his mind. However, he had a business to run and that took precedence over his private life. He was in the process of selling his company to a California firm. When the sale was completed it took him to a level of wealth he could hardly imagine. Regardless of his priorities, he couldn't get away from the impact the petite redhead had made on him.

J.R. continued to invest in various moneymaking schemes. He had invested in the "Bristoe's Buddies" products that consisted of a whole line of toys that a friend of his had invented. They were made popular in the Jackson area because of J.R.'s tireless marketing. It wasn't long until the entire continent knew about "Bristoe's Buddies" because of the exposure on the new media called television. J.R. was one of the first men in the area to promote their line of toys or other products on the fledgling industry. The return on this investment to J.R. was more than he could have ever dreamed. During the same era, he counted among his friends such notable entrepreneurs as Noel Alexander who had founded the Wonder food stores. Although these stores originally were only in Jackson, they soon spread throughout the south. People far and wide could do all their shopping at the "Wonder" store. No one seems to know how the name came about, but it was catchy and easy to remember. Wonder Stores were soon a force to "reckon with" in the grocery business.

The Pritchard-Samson partnership that started the wholesale food company now called Samson Foods were also friends of J.R. They started their business prior to the Depression and managed to stay afloat during the hard times. Their theory was that everyone had to have groceries so they limited their inventory to the staples that all housewives used on a daily basis. That plan kept them in business when others failed. In the early 40s, Pritchard sold his share to Samson and the wholesale food distributor known as Samson Foods was born.

J.R. held a membership in the Petroleum Club that was a private gentlemen's organization during the late 30's and early 40's. This granted him status with the elite of Jackson society and gave him accessibility to ready cash for investments if he needed it. It was not long after these entrepreneurial ventures became lucrative that J.R.Matthews was the one that other inventors came to for resources to fund their ideas. However, it would soon be someone else making the decisions about who got whose money and for what, even if J.R. was the one who earned the money. .

In 1939 when J.R. Matthews met Jewel Treadwell Frederickson, a young mother of two small girls at the Hanson party, it was love at first sight. He was strong, suave, ambitious, and charming. Not since her father died had Jewel met such a captivating man. He was thirty years her senior and whether Jewel knew it or not, she found in him the father image she had lost when her beloved father died some ten years before. Whatever she thought at the time, she was captivated by his very presence. Jewel might have been ready to marry physically, but she was gun shy emotionally since her first marriage had failed so miserably. She was sure that her domineering nature had been the root cause of problems she and Ward had experienced. Therefore she took full responsibility for the disastrous failure. She also was concerned profoundly about any man who would become the stepfather to her daughters. While motherhood had not been her strong suite, she accepted the responsibility and was an excellent mother to the girls. Her concern for their welfare was grounded in the fact that they should always be ladies of good breeding. And that any male influence in their lives should bear that responsibility with her equally. She had known a few women that had remarried but for the reason to end their loneliness, not because the man in their life would make a good father to their children. Jewel was determined not to fall into that category.

J.R. fell in love with Jewel immediately; however, Jewel was not sure she could trust her own judgment and she was not one to be expressive of her feelings. On their third date, J.R. told her that he intended to marry her, but she would have to beg him for at least a year. Jewel smirked at his self-confidence and assured him that she had never begged for anything in her life. He would never get that satisfaction from her. Nevertheless she was a prize to be won. She was a young 26-year-old. She was petite and shapely even though she had borne two children. She was a fashionable and well-bred southern belle. The years as a young divorcee had not changed her character one bit. She loved life and her persona reflected this quality. She could be at ease in any crowd and could handle any situation that came her way with grace and finesse. She had been born into wealth that the trials and traumas of the past had taken away from her, but she had maintained her self-esteem through all the disasters that had befallen her. She never discussed her past with anyone lest they pity her. She was, indeed, a lady of fine breeding. Harvey Treadwell would have been very proud of his daughter and how she had overcome the tragedies of her past. If J.R. thought she was a "catch", he never showed it. He courted her in fine style, and she blended into his circle of friends as if she had always been there. Jewel knew how to be a charming southern belle and she played it to the hilt. Because of his Jackson connections they were invited to all of the society functions of the 40's. Jewel was enchanted by J.R. even though there was a big age difference between them. He was smooth and sophisticated, well liked, and talented in making you feel special. He made Jewel feel special; a characteristic that had evaded her for many years. He loved her dearly and he showed it. Their friends were taken aback by the love light between the two of them. They had an aura that defied explanation. Although he was very wealthy, he never flaunted it. He could be comfortable with the man in the street as well as the richest member of the Petroleum Club. He made no class distinction.

    J.R. was a recent widower. He had been married for several years to his childhood sweetheart. On a winter Sunday morning while she was travelling to church a wayward drunken driver hit his wife's car at an intersection near her home. She was severely injured in the accident but lived a short time before finally succumbing to her injuries. She was able to talk briefly with J.R. before she passed away, but he found little comfort that her young life was snuffed out by someone so careless. They had no children of their own but had adopted a baby girl several years before the accident. In Jackson, at that time, there was a "baby gin" taking place. It seems there were two Judges in Jackson who had put together a scheme whereby pregnant teenagers could sell their unwanted babies to the highest bidders. Because there was no effective birth control in the 30's, there never seemed to be a shortage of unwanted babies born. Many of the babies, at that time, were born at home and there were few records kept of the parents of these children. Judge Sullivan and Judge Gibson were partners in the crime. Some of the babies being sold were of mixed race reportedly the product of rape by black sharecroppers. In the 30's there were many opium addicts in America and the children of these addicts were sold as well. And, even though it was never discussed, many babies were the result of incest. If a mother refused to sleep with her husband because of a fear of another pregnancy, he might find an older daughter who would be forced to satisfy her father's needs. In Leflore County the law did not see this as a crime. Regardless of the circumstances, the babies were sold to anyone who wanted a child but did not want to give birth or couldn't endure a full term pregnancy. The only requirement for a baby was having enough money. J.R. and his wife fell into the trap. Some of their friends were leery of the procedure and expressed some concern that this was not a legitimate enterprise, however, the Matthews' felt the gain was worth the risk. In 1931 they adopted a girl they called Melody. Three months to the day of the adoption, the case of selling babies broke wide open in Jackson and J.R. was forced to believe the warnings his friends had given him. The Judges were indicted and later stood trial for which they were both sentenced to many years in Federal prison. Both were defrocked, never to practice law again. The adoptive parents were offered the chance to void the procedure and return the babies, however J.R. and his wife opted to keep their baby and raise her as if she had been a blood birth of her parents. After the death of his wife, J.R. continued to care for Melody and she went on to follow him in his business ventures.

Many stories were told about J.R. Matthews, about his generosity to the less fortunate and about his sensitivity to animals. One particular story involved an experience he had with his own expensive bird dogs. J.R. spared no money when it came to his hunting hobbies. He purchased the finest dogs available to him and treated them as if they were royalty. He had taken one of his recent purchases to be trained by "Uncle" Ewing Carlton in Leflore County. It seems J.R. had paid a big price for this female. He wanted her to be trained to hunt, and then he thought she should be bred by one of Ewing's well-trained, expensive studs. However, the bitch was very "high strung" and very hard to handle. He attempted to hold her but she got away from him. J.R. watched as his prize dog was slaughtered on the highway right before his eyes. The story goes that this scene reduced the proud man to tears over his loss. He wept, not for the loss of his investment, but for the loss of such a beautiful dog. He was a sensitive man and this experience only endeared him to his friends in Leflore County.

The country was about to enter the war. The war in Europe was already in full swing. Hitler had trampled all over eastern Europe and the conversation at every gathering was what would happen next. Jewel was politically minded and well read. She could hold her own during any of the conversations. She had never been one to sit with the ladies in the parlor, but actively expressed herself in conversations with the gentlemen. She read every newspaper she could get her hands on and listened to the radio constantly. She sometimes felt that she was more informed about what was happening on the war front than some of the men in their group of friends. While she did not initiate a conversation, frequently she was asked her opinion once they discovered she was well versed on the subject of the war. Needless to say Jewel would speak her mind when asked. It was never her style to blend into the woodwork.

Jewel Frederickson and Johnson R. Matthews were married on her 27th birthday in 1941. It is doubtful that Jewel did any begging as he had predicted, but more than likely, it was the other way around, although no one ever commented about what really happened. He had courted her for more than a year and the time was right for both of them to become one. J.R. spared no expense in the things he bought for Jewel. He wanted her to have the best. He felt he was "walking in tall cotton" when he won her hand and expected to make her the grandest lady of the south. They had a beautiful, large, and elaborate wedding attended by the elite of Jackson. All of J.R.'s business associates as well as his friends from the Petroleum Club were in attendance. No expense was spared to celebrate this union. And, to Jewel, she was leaving the poverty of the past behind her, never to look back. A honeymoon trip to New York City was his gift to her. At long last, Jewel could see something beyond Leflore County. She could hardly wait.

Alyce Godbey

CHAPTER FOURTEEN

A Southern Belle

Jewel adapted to the new life style like a duck takes to water. She had gone from rags to riches when she married J.R. It had been a long time since she could enjoy freedom from want as she was about to experience as the new Mrs. Matthews. Little did she know that the best was yet to come!

J.R. continued to invest in business ventures. If he had the "Midas Touch", he also was endowed with the gift of spending. Therefore, Jewel Matthews had everything her little heart desired. He was astounded to discover that Jewel did not want much. She had not inherited her mother's trait of spending. Jewel, on the contrary, "squeezed the nickels until the buffalo yelled", as the saying goes. She was stylish and fashionable but refused to spend money on frivolous things. Her wardrobe was filled with basics and she added her personal touch with a scarf or piece of jewelry when she felt the outfit needed more "pizzazz". She never bought clothes that she felt would be out of style next year. Instead, she concentrated on the things she could wear a long time and yet she could be well dressed no matter where they went. J.R. gave her jewelry for every occasion until she finally asked that he not be so lavish. She preferred simple jewels and not anything ostentatious. He was only too happy to oblige this request. He felt she didn't ask for much so he should honor her wishes. Her one love was to travel and J.R. could handle that request with ease, since he enjoyed travelling too. As a salesman, he traveled a lot to many different cities. He took Jewel to visit as many places in the United States as he could work into his schedule. They did not travel abroad since Jewel felt she preferred to see her own country. After all, she was a country girl at heart and never had any interest in foreign travel especially since most of the foreign nations were at war with each other or with the United States. She had no desire to see war-torn Europe. After all she had seen enough devastation by relating to her own childhood and the fire of her home in 1932.

Jewel insisted on handling their financial affairs. She was skilled at handling money and only needed to reflect back to her days at the gin to remember how important it was to conserve their cash flow. She continued to parlay their income into a fortune. The couple was making money, but they were not stingy. Their philanthropy was legendary and many charities were the recipients of their generosity, as we will see in a later chapter.

On a cold winter Sunday morning in December, 1941, Jewel, J.R. and a group of friends met at the Matthews household with preparations to enjoy an early Sunday brunch followed by their church service. As one of the couples arrived, they had been listening to the car radio and heard the news of the invasion of Pearl Harbor. The entire party spent the morning gathered around the radio to hear President Roosevelt declare war on Japan. J.R. was overwhelmed. He knew he was too old to go to war, but he exclaimed he would join if they would have him. Needless to say, that didn't happen but the Matthews supported the war effort in every way. They bought war bonds in huge amounts – a favorite investment of Jewel's. The held support rallies in their home, Jewel rolled bandages with her friends and they could be seen at any events supporting the troops overseas. From that day forward Jewel's interest in the war effort would consume most of her spare time. She prayed for the troops daily and continued to do so until the day the war was over.

CHAPTER FIFTEEN

Not Dewey

 Jewel's daughters were becoming quite attached to their new stepfather. Belinda was now a grown up seven years old and Yvonne was six. J.R. adored the girls and considered them his own children. He was the only father figure they had ever really known. Their biological father had remarried and had a daughter of his own from that second union. They had not seen him since they had moved to Jackson. Since the day they were born, he had not had any influence on their upbringing. If Jewel would have allowed his influence is an unanswered question. She had complete control over the welfare of the girls and she preferred it that way. When she informed Ward that J.R. wanted to adopt the girls he was very willing to grant his permission. J.R. adopted the girls and became a "hands on" father. In 1943 the Court granted their permission for Belinda and Yvonne Frederickson to change their names to Matthews. It was a big day for everyone. Jewel was ecstatic and the girls would see no change in their lifestyle since they had looked upon him as their father for a long time. J.R. became the loving father and mentor for the girls; spending as much time with them as he could. He taught Belinda the love of history, particularly of the Civil War. Jewel and J.R. were both avid historians and could tell stories of the involvement of their ancestors in the Civil War. These stories came alive when they were expounding on events that happened in Leflore County and surrounding areas. They had just endured the First World War and it was not history yet. It was still too fresh in their memory to be considered anything they wanted to relive. However, the Civil War had many events centered in Jackson and Leflore County. Belinda couldn't get enough of the folklore and facts about that time in history.

After the W. W. II was over the Matthews household settled into a more peaceful lifestyle, that is, until election time. They had been supporters of Franklin D. Roosevelt and were bereaved at his death. Jewel felt he had been too ill to govern for a long time, but she still mourned his passing. Harry Truman had succeeded him in the White House and was sworn in as President shortly after FDR died. Jewel was not quick to accept Truman on face value. She understood he was a common man and would have the interest of the less fortunate at heart. However, she wasn't sure he was up to the challenge. He was from the neighboring state of Missouri and she gave him credit for his heritage since the Midwest needed representation in the White House. When the election came around in 1948, Truman announced that he would seek re-election. Jewel and J.R. decided that Thomas Dewey would make a better president. He was, then, the governor of New York and would have a better idea of handling the country's leadership. He was from a wealthy family and was of good breeding. In their mind's eye, he was more equipped to handle the big business of running the country. They actively campaigned for Dewey in the Jackson area. When he visited the city during his campaign tour, they were there to greet him and to give their contribution. They spent many hours at Republican headquarters working to help him get elected. On the night of the election there was a victory rally held at the Hanson Hotel that was attended by the Matthews. The celebration was a big hoopla and everyone went home with the idea that Thomas E. Dewey was the next president of the United States. Jewel switched on her radio when they were getting ready for bed and heard H. G. Kaltenborn, the noted radio newscaster, mockingly, announce that Harry Truman would soon be returning to Missouri to live out the rest of his life. Mr. Dewey would sleep in peace this evening, knowing he was the president-elect. Imagine their surprise when the morning paper told the real story – Truman had won! The count was very close and indeed, the world thought that Truman was defeated, but it was not to be. Jewel and J.R. were shocked and disappointed, however, true to form, they supported their new president as if he had been their choice from the start.

The girls were growing into young ladies, and they were attending private schools. Since money was no object, J.R. wanted them to have the best education he could buy. They excelled in all of their studies and this fact delighted their parents. The girls had obviously inherited their mother's desire to learn. They were both avid readers and had a book in their hands all the time. Belinda had a flair for the finer things for her home. She loved the architectural aspect of the old houses in their neighborhood. She was fascinated by Civil War history and many of the antebellum homes around Jackson inspired her to study the décor of that time period. Yvonne, on the other hand, preferred to study the Bible. She had an intense interest, no doubt inherited from her mother, to study the Old Testament. She tried very hard to envision the lifestyle of the early prophets and their prophecy of the future. And, at their mother's insistence, the girls were in church for every activity that applied to their age.

Belinda was beginning to show signs of restlessness but at the same time she was a tease to her sister. If she could pull off a prank and not be discovered, she would torment Yvonne until she cried. J.R. traveled a lot and was gone from the house many days. As lunchtime came one Saturday, Jewel insisted the girls gather around the table, bow their heads, and say "grace" together. When all the heads were bowed, Belinda dropped Yvonne's pet goldfish into her glass of milk. No one noticed the dastardly deed until Yvonne had consumed most of the milk. She spied the helpless critter swimming for dear life in the bottom of her glass. Yvonne became hysterical; not only of the loss, but that she had consumed most of the milk that she was sure the fish had poisoned. Jewel tried to calm Yvonne, and frantically attempted to think of a way she could punish Belinda that would fit the crime and at the same time not plunge her into a sullen spell. Jewel could only think that if J.R. had been there he would have handled it better than she did. Finally she instructed Belinda to get her Sunday School lesson book and sit at the table and read it aloud for all to hear. Jewel knew this wasn't much punishment for her mischievous act but she just didn't think she could tolerate any type of sullen attitude from Belinda if she meted out a stronger penalty. Yvonne was promised another goldfish and the day continued.

Belinda was moody and sullen most of the time. She had temper tantrums when things did not go her way. She learned early that she could control most of the family and she used it to her benefit. Jewel had a difficult time coping with this personality trait. She had no patience with her and only could demand her obedience. Belinda, on the other hand, simply rebelled at any form of force from her mother. Jewel could not understand this behavior since she herself was almost never out of sorts. She seemed to be helpless to reach Belinda. She simply did not know what to do to help her. When she tried to enforce a rule, Belinda only rebelled that much more. Jewel found the only way she could deal with her was to ignore her most of the time. She felt obligated to do something, but she just wasn't sure what it should be. J.R. hardly knew what to do either, and they both agreed that she probably would outgrow it. However, it didn't happen that way.

If Belinda presented a problem, Yvonne had her own set of maladies. Yvonne seemed to be sick most of the time. She seemed to have significant digestive problems. She was frail and thin no matter what she ate. She was beset with painful stomachache almost constantly. No amount of home remedying seemed to help and doctors were stymied as to the cause. Because Jewel rarely had a sick day, she could not imagine what illness had befallen Yvonne. After several months of agonizing bouts of stomach pain, J.R. insisted they take her to a doctor whom he knew in New York City for observation. The trip was a wonderful vacation experience for the girls since they had never been out of Jackson for any extended trips. They went by train and as the locomotive rattled along the tracks they could see the towns as they traveled through on their way to the next one. When night came and they climbed into the Pullman car to sleep in the upper berth, they could hardly stop giggling with excitement. Both girls thought that this train ride was the greatest adventure they had ever experienced. And, there would certainly be more of these exciting excursions to follow.

After the doctors had run a number of tests on Yvonne, the consensus of opinions was that she had "Celiac's" disease. The disease is one that affects the lining of the intestine. Everything that has milled flour in it tends to irritate the lining and causes pain. A diet of fruits and vegetables seemed to be the answer, but this also meant she could have no bread, biscuits, cakes, cookies, or other pastries. Such a diagnosis for a child was not good news; however, Yvonne determined that she would not complain. Jewel made a rule in their house; they would never talk about illnesses and always put up a front of good health. Jewel did what she could to make her life as pleasant as possible and Yvonne attempted to abide by the "no complaining" rule, at least in her mother's presence.

Aside from the biological ailment, Yvonne appeared to have some mental disorder. She was unable to make decisions for herself and seemed helpless to do much without explicit direction. No one wanted to state that she was retarded because she seemed to have a high level of intelligence in some areas. However, she seemed unable to live in the normal world. Everything she attempted to do drained her of all her energy and she would be exhausted by noon, leaving the family in a quandary as to what was wrong with her. Doctors did not seem to have the answers since the problem was mental and not physical. A mental problem was not discussed at all, even with family members. Jewel was sure she would remain with her forever since there was not way of teaching her to live in the outside world.

CHAPTER SIXTEEN

The Girls Grow up

As the girls continued to grow, Jewel wanted them to have the best education they could get, since she had so little. Belinda was sent to a private school and Yvonne attended the public school at first but later she joined her sister in the same school. Belinda was difficult to handle in her everyday life. She was moody and high strung at the same time. Some days she was sweet and docile; the next day she would stay in her room all day with the door locked. Jewel considered her a real challenge but continued to mete out the only punishment she knew – ignore her actions. Withdrawing her privileges punished her temper tantrums. Her moodiness was just ignored. Belinda was extremely intelligent, no doubt a trait she had inherited from her mother, but her emotional problems seemed to be the dominant force in her behavior. She was a voracious reader and seemed to have an insatiable quest for knowledge. She spent many hours reading English Literature. Her appetite for English historical novels kept her on a constant trip to the library. She also enjoyed architecture of the Elizabethan era and became a self-taught expert on the subject. She subscribed to various magazines relating to architecture and design. These hobbies were her mainstay of entertainment, and they were apparently enough to keep her mind occupied most of the time. The only time she became a problem was when she was confronted. Her reaction to anyone who disagreed with her was to retaliate with her own brand of rebellion. She withdrew from the scene and retreated into her own world of depression. However, depression was not a treatable malady in the early days of Belinda's life. No doctor seemed equipped to discuss, diagnose or treat depression as a disease. For the most part, Belinda's personality problems went untreated.

Jewel made sure the girls attended church each Sunday and they were very active in the church activities. Yvonne was a serious Bible student and had a thirst for Bible knowledge that was unusual for her age. She spent most of her free time studying the Bible. She had very few friends and preferred to stay indoors with her mother and read whatever she could find that would help her understand the Bible.

As previously noted, in 1943, when J.R. Matthews had adopted the girls; their names were changed to Matthews. A legal adoption was recorded in Rankin County, changing their names to Belinda Matthews and Yvonne Matthews. Church records were changed to show the name change and they were all Matthews now. At about the same time all four of the Matthews moved their church membership to First Christian Church in Jackson.

1951, Belinda was 16 years old and was beginning to notice boys. She was a beautiful girl, with strawberry blond hair and flashing eyes. She loved to dress well, just like her grandmother before her. She admired Berthina and often commented that she wanted to be just like her. Because Belinda was so attractive she was never without an escort to any function at church or school. When she was a senior in high school she was invited to the Prom. This invitation turned into quite an experience. Finding a dress that suited Jewel and Belinda seemed like an impossible task. They shopped at every department store or specialty shop in Jackson but were unable to agree on the style or color. Finally, after looking for the dress for two months, Jewel decided she would have someone make the dress. The fabric was purchased and Belinda chose the style. When the dress was completed Belinda determined she would not wear the dress or attend the Prom. Finally in desperation, Jewel agreed that maybe that was the best avenue to take. On the night of the Prom a young man rang the doorbell with the intention of escorting Belinda to the Prom. It seems she had chosen not to tell him she did not intend to go. At this point, J.R. became involved. He invited the gentleman into the parlor and asked him to wait a few minutes. He then went upstairs to the room where Belinda had attempted to barricade herself in rebellion. He entered the room and stated very succinctly that she <u>would</u> be going to the Prom. It was not his intent to dress her but if it became necessary he certainly would. He made every effort to be patient, however, his anger was hardly disguised. He assured her that no daughter of his would be allowed to behave in this manner and certainly no lady would ever be so rude to a gentleman. Needless to say, the two young people soon left for the Prom together. When they returned home around midnight, the story goes that a good time was had by all. And J.R. never had to enforce the rules with Belinda again.

Before she was 18 years old, Belinda had fallen in love. She was still in school when she met a fellow student, Kenneth Dale. He was a handsome man and a good dresser. His quiet nature tended to be the opposite of the volatile Belinda. His mannerisms displayed a good breeding background, and Jewel accepted this trait as an asset. This dashing young man impressed Belinda, and she loved having him on her arm at any function that she could entice him to attend with her. He had the manners of Valentino and the looks to go with the name. He simply swept Belinda off her feet.

She graduated from High School that spring and before fall was planning a wedding. The ceremony was to be an elaborate affair and it would be held at First Christian Church. The assistant pastor would perform the ceremony. He was a personal friend of Jewel and J.R.'s, and had visited in their home several times. Of course, money was no object for the Matthews and the bash was being planned with as much splash as a coronation of a queen. After all, Belinda thought she was one. Jewel had instilled that thought in her because she was a descendant of the Treadwells of Leflore County. Jewel looked forward to seeing her firstborn marry and the day was one of great anticipation. If miracles still happen, all the plans and details that had gone into the "royal" event had paid off. The wedding went off without a hitch and the bride and groom were married in fine style.

They left immediately for New Orleans on a brief honeymoon. Belinda Matthews Dale never seemed happier.

CHAPTER SEVENTEEN

A Grandmother

Jewel and J.R. were living on Lowell St. in Jackson, and they bought the house next door for the newly-weds. This may not have been the best idea for Belinda and Kenneth Dale. With them under the watchful eye and domineering hand of her mother the newly-weds were overshadowed in their quest for some privacy. Jewel was relieved to see Belinda married off and she readily welcomed Kenneth Dale as a member of the family. He was the knight in shining armor in Jewel's eyes and both his parents and the Matthews's gave their blessings to the couple. However, peace would not come to them.

While Ken and Belinda were getting adjusted to married life, Yvonne was experiencing more health problems. Her intestinal problems seemed to flare up almost unexpectedly no matter what she ate. Jewel continued to attempt to help her with every known remedy and every doctor available. She had constant medical attention but convincing her that the proper diet was important was much more difficult. The Matthews took Yvonne to specialists all over the country in efforts to seek expert medical attention. Some of the treatments helped the situation and others did not. However, the Matthews never ceased to try new and experimental methods in their attempt to alleviate her constant pain. The family enjoyed the travels to various places even though their trips were related to Yvonne's health. Nevertheless the expeditions were exciting. These travels were the manifestation of Jewel's early childhood dreams. She was able to see those far-away places she had once envisioned as she rode her horse on those God-forsaken dirt roads in Leflore County.

Shortly after they were married, Mr. & Mrs. Kenneth Dale announced that Belinda was pregnant. Jewel winced with the news, remembering how she had felt when she received the same kind of information. She was also aware that Belinda was not stable and that the pregnancy might just push her over the edge. Because they lived next door, she could keep a watchful eye on her and foresee any mental problem that might arise. Ken, as he was called, had not been made aware of any mental problems that Belinda had experienced in the past. Everyone had done a marvelous job of hiding any such problems during their courtship. However, Ken was in love and perhaps he simply turned a blind eye to any mood swings she might have had. So when symptoms began to surface, it was news to him. In the beginning, he kept most of the problems to himself, but gradually shared some of them with Jewel. He had no background in handling this type of problem, and he was totally unequipped to handle Belinda's depression. He fell into the same pattern the family had used to treat her, ignore her, maybe the problem will go away. No one was willing to address her problem as "manic depression".

In the winter of 1953, Belinda and Ken became the parents of a bouncing baby boy, named Kenneth Dale, Jr. He was a delight to behold and the proud father could hardly believe he had helped to create such a beautiful baby. He spent as much time with him as he could and delighted in helping with his care. He was the epitome of a good father and he became a good caregiver. Belinda experienced post-partem depression after the birth of the baby and it became Ken's job to take care of her and the baby. He had no idea how to handle Belinda and did the only thing he knew to do; wait on her hand and foot.

Jewel was happy to greet this new creature as her grandchild, and Aunt Yvonne smiled upon this baby as a gift from God. However, because of her frailty she was virtually unable to assist in the care of an infant. She loved the baby but could only watch him from a distance. Yvonne could not change a diaper or feed the baby because she was unable to grasp the task of handling the baby carefully. Belinda was passive about the entire scene of motherhood; but, she took excellent care of the baby and could never have been accused of not being a good mother in her own way. It appeared that she did what the baby did; when he ate, she ate, when he cried, she cried, when he slept, she slept, and so it went; day in and day out.

The news of a newborn in the family was great news however, it would be only temporary. In the mail came the notice that Ken Sr. would be drafted into the war effort. It was the time of the

Korean War and most young men had already been called to service. Although Ken was a father, that did not grant him hardship status. He was called to do his basic training in Ft. Leonard Wood Missouri and he left his wife and baby at home. Basic training at the base was rigorous and tough on a man who had never worked in a farm field, planted or picked cotton, or had to shovel coal in the mines. He complained bitterly but to no avail. Upon graduation from basic training he was given the opportunity to choose his next assignment. He really had no idea but quickly opted for something he thought would be inside and a desk job. He asked to be assigned to the Missile Training Center at Los Alamos, New Mexico. It was far from home, but he would have furloughs when he could return to Jackson to visit. Maybe he could even take Belinda and Ken Jr. with him. The opportunity to pursue his career choice and go to Los Alamos presented itself in full force, and Ken Sr. was shipped off within the week. He had to undergo extreme testing and was finally given a top-secret clearance to work in the Logistics and Supply in the Los Alamos compound.

Ken Sr. was barely settled in at Los Alamos and trying to get acclimated to his new job when, on his first call home, Belinda gave him more good news. She was pregnant again. Ken hardly knew what to say. He loved his baby but wondered how she could handle two babies without his help. He knew that Jewel would help all she could but he needed to be there. However, the Army had other ideas. Try as he might, he was unable to get a "hardship" transfer to a base closer to home. No, the Army needed him right where he was and Belinda would have to manage. Before Ken, Jr. was 2 years old the proud parents were to welcome the second son, whom they named John. Ken Sr. would travel home on leave as often as he could afford it. When he needed to make the trip to settle some matter at home, Jewel would send him enough money to fly home. Although each time he came home it seemed he spent his time "putting out fires" and trying to help Belinda adjust to life in his absence. And, it appeared that each time he had a furlough and came home, Belinda became pregnant. Ken Sr. wanted to move his family to New Mexico however Jewel fought that idea. She was sure that she would lose control of them if they went out west. Since his service time would soon be up, she convinced him that the family was better off in Jackson where she could help them when they needed it. Soon after the birth of Johnny, the third son would follow, named Arthur. In a short 5 years, Belinda and Ken, Sr. had 3 sons. Ken Sr. soon returned home to handle the affairs of his family and to tend to the needs of Belinda who seemed to drift into depression more often than usual. He kept most of the problems to himself and rarely discussed any of Belinda's health problems with Jewel for fear of incurring her wrath. She was sure she knew how to handle Belinda and she didn't intend to let anyone else tell her she was wrong.

Jewel was not at all happy about this procreativity taking place and she said so. She continually made every effort to enforce her rules and regulations on the burgeoning family. Belinda had not listened to Jewel before, and she had no intention of hearing from her now. Money was tight for the ever-growing family and it never seemed to stretch far enough. Jewel was always ready with another handout but surely felt that if she was supporting them she could control them too. Ken had an opportunity to go to work in an insurance company and was starting to do well, financially. If he had only to support himself and Belinda he would have been making an adequate salary, but there never seemed to be enough money for so many hungry mouths. Money became a constant need in the household, and their ability to manage their money seemed non-existent. To survive on their own income would have been a real challenge but the on-going demand for the good life took away most of their income. They had domestic help since Belinda had never known any other procedure except to "have the nanny do it." And she was mentally unstable to the point that she was unable to cope with the day to day routine of three boisterous sons. They insisted on the best of everything from the food they ate to the décor in their home. Belinda loved the finer things of life and she was determined to have them regardless of the strain on the budget.

Before the first child went to school, Belinda was pregnant again. This time she gave birth to a girl named Jennifer. At last, there would be a girl child in the household. If Belinda felt that they had enough babies or whether Kenneth Sr., realized his limitations of raising this brood, they announced that this would be their last. Jewel held her own celebration for this announcement. She loved the babies as much as any grandmother, however, she feared for Belinda's health and the eventual outcome of the upbringing of the children.

If the repeated pregnancies affected her mental condition will never be known, but Belinda continued to have good days and bad days. Sometimes she could hardly get out of bed, and other days she was very active, taking part in the children's activities. They were in as many events at school and church as they could manage. With the help of Ken Sr., Yvonne, Jewel, and the hired help, the children enjoyed a well-rounded childhood.

In 1958, Jewel and J.R. bought the house at 1930 Hanson St., just a few blocks from the Dale household. They gave the house they were living in to the Dale family. Belinda and Ken promptly moved into the house her mother had occupied. It was a bigger house and had a fenced-in yard where the children could safely play. And the growing family needed the extra room to spread out in if for no other reason than to be out of their mother's reach. To assist them financially, Jewel deeded the property to Belinda and Ken, Sr. and continued her almost constant support of them. They promptly sold the smaller home and spent the money. No one will ever know whether there were monstrous bills to pay or if they simply wanted money in their pocket, nevertheless they felt the money was theirs. Jewel still had the idea that you should not sell property, but no doubt the Dale's saw it differently. They considered the property a gift and the set out to enjoy their newfound wealth. Regardless of their thought process, they enjoyed the money and squandered it all on "frivolous things", according to Jewel.

If the pressures of being a young father of four active children, the demands of being a fledgling insurance agent, or dealing with Belinda on a daily basis were the reasons, it may never be known, the facts were that Kenneth Dale Sr. had become a closet drinker. He had always been comfortable with a little "nip" here and there.

Now it was a full-fledged drinking habit. He was not a "partying" type of drunk. He was not a roaring drunk but quietly, drank himself into oblivion most evenings. There were scenes when Ken would be in the bathtub drinking and be so overcome with the effects of alcohol that he was unable to get out of the tub. The boys were then enlisted to help their mother move their dad into bed to sleep it off. If the truth were told, Belinda probably objected to this type of behavior. She had never experienced any type of alcohol as a child growing up, but had heard the stories of her step-grandfather "Dr. Franke", from her grandmother. She knew full well the attitude of the Treadwell family about such behavior. But because she feared her mothers' reprimand, she seldom mentioned it to her. No doubt she felt that was the best line of action to take. Who knows what would have happened if Jewel had known the truth about the man that she considered a "knight in shining armor".

Emotions ran high at the Dale household, and money became the topic of conversation on a daily basis. Jewel continued to dole out the cash as needed for the family. Ken continued his drinking sometimes becoming abusive to Belinda. If he was not physically abusive, it was certainly mental abuse, and considering her depressive nature, it would take its toll on her eventually. He felt she was the cause of most of their problems. He didn't see his drinking as a root cause or even an obstacle to family harmony. He seemed oblivious to the fact that he could have done more to alleviate the traumatic situation in the home. However he seemed helpless to change any of the circumstances including his own behavior. The children grew in this chaotic atmosphere and the effects on them would be evident in the future. Jewel continued to buy off on any personal needs that she was made aware of and the lifestyle of her oldest daughter never changed.

CHAPTER EIGHTEEN

Jewel Buys the Cabin

Jewel, Yvonne and J.R. were enjoying their life together. There was a lot of traveling to doctors seeking treatment for Yvonne, and they took many pleasure trips to help satisfy Jewel's need for adventure. J.R. also had several business interests that took him to all parts of the country. They visited nearly every metropolitan city in the United States. Jewel delighted in these jaunts and lived the life of a socialite wife. Even though she was traveling to many exciting places, Jewel had not forgotten her roots in Leflore County. It had gnawed at her that the bank, during the Great Depression, had repossessed the Treadwell land. Even though she had consented to sell a lot of the land back in the 30s, she mourned that loss as if it were a sibling. She resented the foreclosures and considered them a blot on the family history. She felt the name of her beloved father had been tarnished. And she ultimately blamed Berthina for being so careless in her management of the properties her husband had left to her. Jewel knew her father felt he was providing for his family by owning land. Harvey would never know that Berthina was so ill equipped to handle this type of legacy. She had little or no knowledge of any way to use the inheritance to provide for her and Jewel. Jewel never got over the fact that all the land had gone to someone other than a Treadwell. In 1959 she heard that one of the current owners had his property for sale. She viewed this as an opportunity to fulfill the promise she made to her dying father. Jewel consulted her good friend, Charlie Stanton, and authorized him to purchase the property for her. She was not a foolish investor. She knew the value and intended to get the property at a good price. Charlie Stanton did not disappoint her. He held out for the bottom dollar price and made Jewel a happy landowner. The purchase marked the beginning of Harvey Treadwell's family returning as landowners in Leflore County. Her first purchase was the plot of ground that had the cabin and the overseer's house on it. To Jewel, this was the most prized purchase of her life and it was not to be the last time she would buy part of Leflore County. Now she could say she had a home in Leflore County. The part of the farm that lay across the road from the cabin that she had just purchased still had a barn and stable on it. Jewel quickly bought two horses and had them stabled there. She had in her mind that she would return to the cabin and go horseback riding from time to time. She had never lost her love for horses although she hadn't been on one for many years. She could still remember her horse, Lance, and the many times she spent riding him. One of the most memorable times she remembered in horror was the day they rode home from school and discovered their home was on fire. She also had fond memories of the colt that Lance had sired. She was there the night the colt was born and helped the vet handle the birthing process. She promptly named the horse Nancy after Nancy Drew, the heroine in her favorite books.

J.R. never restricted Jewel's purchase of investments. He knew she had a 6th sense about her when it came to buying properties. While he was never in love with the cabin in Black Hawk, he humored Jewel and allowed her to establish a residence there for their enjoyment away from the city. They went to the cabin often where Jewel could enjoy the countryside away from the hustle and bustle of Jackson. It was also a wonderful place to take Yvonne when she was not in good health. She seemed to be more comfortable "at the farm" than in the city.

Jewel never spent money on creature comforts. When they bought the house on Hanson St., they were buying into the elite section of Jackson at that time. Their neighbors were none other than E.H. Stanton, the uncle of Jewel's attorney, and the former mayor of Jackson. While it was a comfortable house, it was not lavish. The developer who had built the Hanson neighborhood homes had built the one the Matthews bought for himself. It was of the "Mission Style" with massive doors and lead bound windows. The archways and openings inside the house were all framed with large oak planks finished to a glossy sheen with dark wood stain. The fireplace was marble imported from Italy to suit the wife of the developer for her own home. Jewel loved the house from the first glance and felt the large back yard would give the feel of being in the country. She had purchased some quality furniture prior to their move but the former owner had left many of the furnishings in the house. She added a few pieces of her own taste, but considered the furniture the former owner had owned to be good enough for her. Her kitchen was just as it had been for many years, with an outdated sink that hung on wall complete with a muslin curtain around it to hide the plumbing. She kept her priceless china in a butler's pantry behind a makeshift door. Jewel felt it was suitable; after all, she wasn't going to cook there anyway. She had a maid for that. She had once commented that if she had to choose one thing above all else to have, it would be a cook. The home had a small porch on the back of the house that was completely open. Jewel thought it would be nice to have it screened in so the family could enjoy the outdoors without the bugs and mosquitoes. She mentioned her idea to J.R. and his response was that he thought it was not necessary and too small to make a comfortable living area. While he was gone on a business trip to Dallas, Texas, Jewel had a contractor enclose the porch and install screens and a door that would lock. When J.R. returned from his trip, she awaited him on the porch in her rocker. He came to the doorway, glanced all around the newest addition and commented: "now, who wouldn't enjoy this lovely porch". The subject of the porch was never discussed again, and true to Jewel's prediction; the family did enjoy the porch away from flying insects.

Jewel was a savvy hostess. She could throw out a lavish dinner party with all the trappings of any society belle. She had sterling silver, fine crystal, and imported china, all to be used on linen tablecloths and napkins with silver candelabra adorning the table. Nothing was left undone when it came to the proper table setting. Her hired help was the finest she could hire and their job was to make the party a success. It was a work of art to turn out those parties with the limited equipment that Jewel had in the kitchen. However, she insisted the kitchen was sufficient and the cook needed to know how to make it all happen. If that was the "order of the day", the cook better be able to rise to the challenge.

The Hanson Street house had four bedrooms, all on the second level. One full bathroom was on the upper level and a half bath was located about three steps below the living area in the lower part of the house. The half bath served as the powder room for visitors who came to the house. There was no bath or bedroom on the main level of the house. Jewel never changed this configuration noting that it worked for her so it would have to work for everyone else. If the house on Hanson was outdated, the cabin in Leflore County was beyond primitive. The floors of the cabin were covered with the original linoleum, the bath was a converted porch with a makeshift shower, the lighting consisted of bare bulbs hanging from the ceiling, the air-conditioning was open windows, the heat in the winter was provided by a roaring fire in the fireplace, and the doors fit so poorly that a brisk breeze through the door frames gave the fireplace a run for its money. In fact, Harvey Treadwell had seen the cabin the same way in 1929. There was a wood cook stove in the kitchen and Jewel expected the cooks to use it summer and winter. When most of the cooks Jewel hired didn't know how to cook on a wood stove, Jewel had to be convinced that an electric stove would produce less heat in the summer and be more efficient for baking pies. It was a big sacrifice on Jewel's part to accept the fact that no one, except her, could test the heat in the oven with her hand or know just how much wood to use to make the oven hot enough for a meal of biscuits and gravy. Jewel could whip up that kind of breakfast in a flash but for the hired help to make a meal on the old range became a near miracle. An electric range was installed in the cabin and Jewel pretended it had always been there.

J.R. was not a well man. At age 74, his health was failing. He was still working on his business interests and Jewel was busily investing every penny she could get her hands on. She had purchased property in old East Jackson. She managed to secure a ninety-nine year lease on the property from a large business developer. The lease had changed hands several times, but Jewel continued to collect rent without ever leaving home. She always rented the property with the idea the new tenant could do his own updating. Her leases had a built-in "cost of living clause" so she was assured of an increase in rent without further negotiations. She also had purchased a piece of ground in a small northern town in Mississippi. She had a building erected on the property and promptly leased it the United States Postal Service for the new post office. They signed a one-hundred-year lease and she collected rent for many years. That lease had a "cost of living clause" also and all negotiations were handled in the beginning. When the postal service decided to close the post office in the community, they bought out the lease and Jewel smiled all the way to the bank. She also invested in the stock market and wisely bought and sold stocks that were successful. She seemed to have an uncanny sense about when to invest and when to sell. When others seemed to be caught by a sudden change in the market, Jewel would state that she had sold that part of her stock about two weeks prior to the fall. J.R. had little or no interest in how the money was spent. He felt he could make it and she could invest it, therefore; they were a good pair.

    J.R. had never been a professing Christian until he met Jewel. He always said that he had not had time to become a Christian. Jewel had other ideas. She had brought him to First Christian Church with her and he was sincerely interested in learning about what he had missed most of his life – the blessings that come with being a believer. After a short time he became a born again Christian. He was baptized and continued in the faith until his death. They were active in their church and he had taken an active part in the church activities. When his health began to fail him, Jewel's friend. Dr. Sarver, the pastor at First Christian came to visit J.R. on a weekly basis. He enjoyed J.R.'s intellect and often engaged in deep spiritual conversations with him. For a man who had spent most of his life outside the faith, J.R. absorbed the Christian teachings like a sponge and seemed to have an insatiable thirst for knowledge of the Bible. Many visiting preachers and missionaries had walked through the door at the house on Hanson St. and J.R. relished their conversations and experiences. When the church needed a place for a visitor to stay they knew they would be welcomed at Jewel and J.R.'s house. On one occasion, Jewel was expecting a large crowd for a sit-down dinner in the dining room. Prior to the event, she had fallen and broken her right wrist. She had a brace on it to prevent any further injury. On the night of the party she had several volunteers helping her in the kitchen. Jewel, in her own inimitable fashion, insisted that she could handle some of the preparations of the dinner herself.

As she was taking a large platter of baked chicken with sauce to the dining room, she stumbled and dropped the entire entree' down the front of the buffet. Chicken, sauce and platter went everywhere on the floor. Jewel promptly dropped to her knees, gathered up the chicken, scooped up the sauce in her hands, and with her linen napkins, wiped up the mess from the furniture and the floor. She returned to the kitchen to face a nearly hysterical group of helpers. They were frantically looking for something else to prepare in a hurry. They wondered just what their next move might be. Jewel calmly put the food all on a new platter and announced that it would be served. In words plain and simple she stated, in a now famous line, "them that will, will, and them that won't, won't! Needless to say, the entire meal was consumed and no one made mention of the fact that for once in their lifetime they had eaten food off the floor.

J.R. was an avid dove and quail hunter. He and his friends always planned a hunting trip during dove season. It had been their habit for more than twenty years. In the fall of 1955, the newspaper ran an article stating that Lawrence Welk would be visiting in Jackson for a limited engagement in October. Jewel consulted their friends and they all planned to attend the concert. They purchased their tickets well in advance and made arrangements to dine together before the concert. Just prior to the day, Jewel realized the concert would be held during dove season. She immediately cancelled her inclusion in the group. Amid complaints from the others, she calmly stated that J.R. had done so much for her, the least she could do was grant him his wish to go dove hunting. Lawrence Welk would have to wait.

Keeping the Promise

In 1959 as winter approached, J.R's health continued to deteriorate. He was under constant doctor's care and it appeared that his body was just wearing out. He was still able to function but Jewel realized that he would not be with her much longer. She had loved him deeply. He was the love of her life and she could hardly imagine life without J.R. She tried to focus on the good part of their life together. She could remember with clarity the many trips they had taken together. She looked upon his strength in her life as the Biblical "master of his own household", a trait she had not seen since her father. Jewel was strong in her own right, but she knew when to stand back and let J.R. be in charge. He was a born leader and his ability to handle the leadership role in their family amazed her. She had never known such a great problem solver. She drew from him all these strengths. Jewel had deep spiritual perception. She had faced many tragedies in her life, yet she knew, and would say so to anyone, God was in charge of her life. She had given her life to God when she was a young girl. In the past, when she had strayed from Him, she knew enough to repent and ask for God's forgiveness. She, then, would forge ahead in renewed fellowship and follow His teachings with a new perspective. She tried very hard to live a godly life each day. Although losing J.R. would be a great loss to her, God would bring her through this experience, as He had all the others. She would move ahead with new vigor pursuing any new plans the Lord would have for her.

J.R. died in the early spring of 1960. The funeral was a beautiful service with many of J.R's business partners and acquaintances in attendance. Dr. Sarver held the service at First Christian Church for the huge, overflowing crowd. While Jewel and others mourned the passing of a great husband, father, and community minded citizen, the service had a deep spiritual meaning expressed by Dr. Sarver about his friend. He would be missed by a vast number of friends as well as his two daughters and his faithful wife. Jewel had never been one to show any emotions openly. This event would be no different. Jewel handled the loss with finesse and chose to mourn on her own terms.

CHAPTER NINETEEN

Life as a Widow

Jewel returned to the house on Hanson to continue her life and to care for Yvonne. Her health did not improve much and while she had a brilliant mind, she had serious emotional problems. Her mind didn't seem to be able to handle everyday life, as other people knew it. She was unable to make any decisions or do even the smallest things for herself. She didn't have the ability to handle mundane things such as watering the flowers or fixing their lunch. Part of the problem might have been that Jewel never allowed her to do anything for herself and part of it could have been that there had always been hired help to do it if Jewel didn't do it. No matter the reason, Yvonne was virtually a prisoner in her own frail body. Her mother made all decisions for her whether it was for her clothing or hairstyles or when to take a shower. Yvonne had always had a small dog, but even taking care of her pet was something she could not do alone.

Jewel had learned to drive at the age of 10, and from that day on, always had a car of her own. After J.R's death, Jewel and Yvonne went to the cabin in Leflore County often. They loved it there and, as long as Julia, the cook, went with them, it was a great vacation. Jewel was still a young woman and driving a car to go where she needed to go was not a problem for her. She and Yvonne went wherever they wanted to go, but their wishes were small. They never ventured far from home with the exception of going to Danville to see Percy, Jewel's half brother. He had lived there for several years. The trip to see Percy was an excursion and one Jewel loved to take. She never seemed reticent to get in her car and drive anywhere she wanted to go. They continued to host the visiting clergy from First Christian Church when there was a need to board someone for the night or for a week. Jewel loved the feeling of having someone around her with a love of the Lord.

Jewel and Yvonne continued to live in the house on Hanson St. during the winter and stayed in the cabin at the farm most of the summer. Jewel never talked about how much she missed J.R. but she never again entertained the idea of another marriage. At the age of 46, Jewel Treadwell Frederickson Matthews was, once again, by herself and forced to face the world and all it had to offer.

CHAPTER TWENTY

Berthina Comes Home

By the late 60's Berthina had been married to Mr. Rainey for several years. Their marriage had been a happy one, satisfying the needs for both of them. He catered to her every whim. She likened her life with Mr. Rainey to the one she had enjoyed with Harvey. Once again, she was able to have the material things that she desired. Berthina always had "Cadillac" tastes and Mr. Rainey was financially able to accommodate her. They were socially active in the community and that suited Berthina's tastes. She had always wished to be a society lady and now she had the chance to fulfill that dream. Mr. Rainey was a handsome man for his age and Berthina was still a lovely lady. Together they made a dashing pair no matter where they went. There were many activities at First Christian Church where they attended regularly and the two of them took part in many events until their health would no longer allow them to be so involved.

In 1967 Mr. Rainey became very ill. The doctors gave a serious prognosis in that he probably would never recover. As had been predicted, Mr. Rainey passed away leaving Berthina Foxe Treadwell Franke Rainey a widow for the second time. She inherited enough money to make her happy for a while however; her spending habits were hard to keep in check. She was a very vain woman and spent a great deal of the time primping and pampering herself. She had maintained a youthful and statuesque look about her for her age. And her wardrobe would rival that of any wealthy woman. She wore her age and status quite well until she could no longer take care of herself. .

In 1968, Berthina was in her late 70's, and she was not well. She could no longer live alone. Jewel opened her home to her mother even though the air between them was no better than it had ever been. The roles suddenly became reversed; Jewel became the mother and Berthina became the child. And to further complicate the arrangement, Berthina was not an easy housemate. She complained constantly about her aches and pains, a habit Jewel had never tolerated. Yvonne was not well, and Berthina felt she had to take over the care of her, even though she was scarcely able to take care of herself. Jewel would never allow anyone to assume the role of caregiver for Yvonne and so the household seemed to be in constant chaos. Jewel and Berthina were frequently in disagreement with each other about almost everything, making the Matthews household anything but peaceful. Jewel was thrifty to a fault although she had plenty of money. Berthina was a spendthrift who would have spent her entire inheritance from Mr. Rainey the first month after his death, if Jewel had not stepped in to handle the money for her. Jewel knew her mother could not live alone or manages her own affairs, yet she sometimes resented the disruption in her home. On one occasion there was a heated disagreement over an order for a new dress that Berthina had made through the Sears Catalog. The package had arrived C.O.D. and Berthina expected Jewel to pay the delivery driver for the package. Jewel questioned the order and the package. When she was not satisfied with the explanation, she refused the delivery. Berthina came charging down the steps of the house in a rage. "How could she deny her the pleasure of a new dress", she screamed at Jewel? When Jewel explained that she didn't feel she needed the dress, the price was exorbitant, and where did she expect to wear such a fancy frock? The ensuing argument ended with the attempt by Berthina to strike Jewel as if she were a wayward child. Jewel fended off her open palm and offered her mother a fresh cup of coffee to calm her down. Berthina was not to be placated and retreated to her room to pout. Jewel was a good Christian woman and knew she had an obligation to care for her mother. She knew it would not be easy, but as long as Berthina lived in her home, Jewel provided the best care she knew how to give. She hired the best doctors to care for her and she provided the means to pay the medical bills for her. And she kept a civil tongue as often as she could. Her mother died in 1980 in the home of her only daughter. Although Jewel and Berthina had never had a close relationship as a mother-daughter should, in the end Jewel mourned her passing and had some regrets that she had not done more to foster a more loving companionship with her mother. When she was younger, Jewel harbored a lot of resentment toward Berthina because of her inability to save the property her father had left them. Jewel reasoned that she did the only thing she knew to do at that time. It was her hope that she had atoned for those early mistakes by giving of herself to Berthina when she needed it most. It was still a bitter struggle for her to remember the loss of the farm. She felt her mother did not try to save it from foreclosure. She tried not to think of the times when they were so destitute and the only asset they had was the farm which had fallen into default at the bank. She wanted to erase from her mind the times when they sold a parcel of land only to receive a pittance for her father's investment. She wanted to remember the good times they had enjoyed in the big house before the fire. And when she remembered the times the family had shared a Sunday dinner around the big old round table, heavily laden with food, she was overcome with mixed emotions. These were good times in her life, but also bad times as they signaled, in her memory, the sadness and loss of her father. At this time in her life, Jewel knew she could not look back. Her Christian values mandated that she forgive Berthina and continue her life in peace.

CHAPTER TWENTY-ONE

More of LeFlore County

Jewel kept a keen eye on the happenings in Leflore County. Each time a piece of property from the original Harvey Treadwell farm went on the market, Jewel's attorney, Charlie Stanton notified her. Mr. Stanton had become quite a successful attorney since the days when a sixteen-year-old Jewel Treadwell came to his office to ask his advice. At that time she queried him of how to sell the land of her father. Now she wanted advice on how to buy it back. Mr. Stanton had become a very successful and distinguished lawyer and was well known around Jackson as well as in Leflore County. He knew before he called Jewel that she would buy any land previously owned by her father but Jewel was not an easy buyer. She was shrewd and thrifty with her money. She could not be fooled into buying and paying just any price. She knew the market value. If the seller thought she would pay an exorbitant price because she was a Treadwell, he thought wrong! She only paid what the farm was worth or less, if she could buy it that way. Many times she turned away for the moment with the feeling that no one else would pay the asking price either. She gambled that she would eventually win the waiting game. Little by little, or piece by piece, Jewel had purchased a lot of the old farm. And she had her eye on the rest. Time was on her side and she held on for the chance to own it all. Only then would she have honored the promise to her father.

Jewel and Yvonne spent most of the summers at the cabin on the farm, going down from Jackson before the first Sunday in May, which was "homecoming" at the Mt. Pleasant church. It was tradition on this special Sunday that there would be a big celebration and many of the older members of the church would come for the service and stay for the noon meal. In the South, a "carry-in" dinner is a big event and the array of cakes and pies as well as meat and vegetables would easily have fed most of the community of Black Hawk. These traditions are continued throughout the South and this area was no different than the thousands of others who celebrate in the same way. Jewel and Yvonne usually stayed all summer at the farm. If for some reason they could not remain at the cabin they would return in the fall for the Sunday school celebration on the second Sunday of September. From the day she purchased the cabin until the year 2000, Jewel Matthews never missed either of these events. She generously supported the church and, the local gentry said, they could tell Jewel had visited the church when they counted the money in the collection plate. Jewel never forgot the day she became a Christian. She became a born again Christian right in the pews of the Mt. Pleasant Christian Church in 1924. Her life had been a continual witness to that experience and would continue so until the day she died.

CHAPTER TWENTY-TWO

Belinda Defies Her Mother

Jewel's grandchildren were growing into young adulthood. Each child had developed its own personality. The boys were in high school and had pursued a gardening type of trade. They had loved the farm life of their granny and seemed to adapt to farming on a small scale in the city. They visited Jewel often and loved to hear her stories of how life was in her day. She enjoyed having them, but felt they were not being raised to her satisfaction. Somehow Jewel felt she could rule everyone from her mother to her grandchildren. She continually doled out money to pay expenses for the Dale family. They never seemed to have enough to keep them going. Ken's insurance business was making good money but somehow the expenses always exceeded the income. His drinking had not abated and their lifestyle appeared to be out of control. Belinda and Ken were not getting along very well, and Jewel always seemed to be in the middle of their disputes. She rarely took the side of her daughter, but defended Ken in any confrontation that arose between them. It was apparent that she never had all the facts about the problems and she reacted only on what information she could glean from the children. If she had any opportunity to speak her mind she would do so. Sometimes she wasn't asked to give her opinion and she gave it anyway. In any sense of the word, Jewel meddled in their affairs. The kids seemed to be caught in the middle and ran to their granny for comfort. Jewel enjoyed the role of granny especially since she could hand out money to them and it almost became a bribe. Money for information about the inside happenings in the home was Jewel's method of operation. This didn't seem to be a good idea, but it seemed to be the only way of keeping abreast of what went on at Belinda's house.

By 1979 the tension was almost unbearable in the Dale household. The atmosphere was so volatile that it was noticeable to everyone who knew them. Belinda was very dissatisfied with her marriage and that only caused her depression to spin out of control. Whether her dissatisfaction was due to Ken's continued drinking, the stress of family responsibilities, or her mental state, the facts were that the marriage was crumbling. When they sold the house on Lowell St. and moved over to Veolla St., Jewel had provided the funds for the purchase. If she thought a bigger house nearer her and Yvonne would make the situation better, she was ill advised. Belinda and Ken, again, sold their house and spent the money. Neither of them could manage their finances and that probably contributed to a lot of internal bickering. If they could get their hands on money, it ran through their fingers like rainwater. In all the years they had been married Ken had never been the one to make decisions but he was beginning to realize that someone needed to make some sort of move toward solving the problems.

On a fall day in 1979, Belinda visited her mother and related to her that she intended to file for a divorce. She felt the children were grown enough to handle this decision. She apparently had given some thought to the decision since she had announced her concern for the welfare of the children. Jewel immediately chastised her for even thinking of doing such a thing. She cited all the Biblical reasons why the sanctity of marriage should be preserved. She felt that Belinda should remain with Ken no matter what the eventual cost would be. Jewel could vividly remember the trauma of her own divorce many years before. She could not bring herself to give voice to the thoughts that ran through her mind when she contemplated her own decision to divorce Ward Frederickson. In retrospect she may have been premature and against her own biblical faith when she agreed to her own divorce. And perhaps she, at last, realized her own part in the destruction of her marriage. As she listened to her oldest daughter planning to destroy a faltering family, Jewel could only state that she felt an imperfect marriage was better than no marriage at all. She cited every reason she could think of with the hope Belinda would rethink the situation. Instead, Belinda flew into a rage and screamed mercilessly at her mother. She accused her of constantly meddling in their affairs; blaming Jewel for the continued problems they were experiencing. She reiterated how Jewel had always been in the middle of every argument the Dales had. She mentioned how hurt she was when her mother had taken Ken's side of any dispute. She implicated her in their continuing financial needs, stating that if Jewel had not continually baled them out of debt, perhaps they would have learned to be better managers. They had never had to learn to manage on their own financial abilities because Jewel was always there with a checkbook. Belinda, in a fit of rage, told her mother she would have divorced Ken many years before if Jewel had not continually sided with Ken each time she tried to discuss any problems with her. The guilt that Jewel placed on her had taken its toll on her depressive nature. She felt entirely betrayed by her mother and reminded her that she, too, had sought a divorce many years before leaving her without a father in her childhood when she really needed one. The confrontation was a complete shouting match with each side accusing the other of past incriminations and only culminated when Belinda bolted out of the house, slamming the door behind her, and vowing never to return. She stayed true to her word. She has never darkened her mother's door again. Jewel retreated into her own reverie. She had many regrets about her past treatment of Belinda however the die had been cast. Jewel simply had no knowledge or experience in handling a "manic depressant". If she had been knowledgeable of the disease, perhaps the outcome would have been different. No amount of apologies or atonement would change the status of her relationship with her oldest daughter.

In 1981 Kenneth Dale made a decision. This had never been his forte' He was never one to make decisions easily. He usually followed Jewel's thinking when any confrontation demanded an answer. It will never be known just what actually convinced him that he should make the move he made, but he ventured to see old

Charlie Stanton and sued Belinda for a divorce. He agreed to pay a sizeable amount of spousal support as well as child support for the remaining children at home. She received the house in which she lived since Jewel had given it to her. It was free of any mortgage and Belinda would receive from Ken enough money to buy her the things her vanity required. Ken continued to support the children and to see that they got an education with very little input from his ex-wife. He continued to stay in contact with Jewel visiting her and Yvonne almost weekly. Whether he genuinely came to see her or whether he knew she would support him financially was always a question. However, over the years he became the one person Jewel could depend on to help her if she needed it.

CHAPTER TWENTY-THREE

Jewel Falls

At this time in her life, Jewel was beginning to slow down. She was in her late 60's and she and Yvonne had lived alone for many years. She was experiencing some hip problems but refused to discuss the situation with the family. She steadfastly stuck to her rule of not talking about your ailments to anyone. One evening, as she was coming up the short flight of stairs from the bathroom, she stumbled and fell, hitting her hip on the edge of the stairs. Yvonne attempted to help her mother to get up but Jewel steadfastly refused her assistance. She convinced herself that it was just a bruise and that it would feel better in the morning. Somehow she thought her hip would heal itself overnight. She instructed Yvonne to bring her a pillow and she laid on the steps all night and all the following day. She continued to believe the pain would go away. Yvonne, in desperation, walked to her sister's house and asked for help. She simply said their mother had fallen. Belinda peeked out the door and replied that she would not come to help her. She refused to even listen to the circumstances surrounding Yvonne's need for help. Before Yvonne could complete her explanation Belinda shouted that if Jewel died, they shouldn't expect her to come to the funeral. Yvonne returned home crestfallen and bewildered. She called on Kenneth Sr., and they forcefully took Jewel to the hospital for treatment that evening. Jewels maintained that it was only bad bruise or, at the worst, a sprain. The doctors, however, gave her the diagnosis that her hip was badly broken. She returned home and faithfully did the rehabilitation that the physicians had prescribed. It wasn't long before Jewel had to have hip replacement surgery. Did the 36 hours on the cold floor aggravate the problem? Probably! But Jewel Matthews was a very stubborn and no one could have convinced her that she needed the services of a doctor. She adamantly refused to listen to any one else. She later had to have hip surgery the second time because the first treatment did not heal properly. Jewel faithfully followed the doctors' orders with the exercises that they had given her to do. She exercised each morning and in time regained the use of her hip completely, much to the surprise of everyone. While Yvonne was unable to assist her mother and Belinda refusing to help, Jewel was forced to do for herself. But each time she was hospitalized, it was Kenneth Sr. who came to her rescue. He was the only help available to her and she knew she could depend on him.

Alyce Godbey

CHAPTER TWENTY-FOUR

The Vietnam War

During the late sixties and early seventies Jewel could hardly believe what was taking place in America. It was a tumultuous time for everyone. Jewel's grandchildren were part of the "hippie" generation. No one in the Dale family agreed with the war in Vietnam. They discussed the situation with their grandmother on many occasions. The consensus of opinion was that we shouldn't be there, but we were. Because Jewel had lived through World War II and had been a part of the Korean War through Ken Sr., she had a better understanding of the situation than the grandchildren. She freely gave them her views and experiences and, no doubt, some advice. It was a delightful time for the boys who loved to hear their granny talk about the War, but they had little concept of what a war in that part of the world meant. Kenneth Jr. and Johnny were protestors against the involvement of the United States in the war. Ken Jr. went to San Francisco as part of a group of "flower children" and remained there. Johnny participated in the protest marches in

Washington, D.C. and seemed completely involved in the effort to avoid the war. The draft was in full force in 1971, Arthur decided his number was bound to come up soon so he went to the Selective Service office and volunteered to be an inductee. Not knowing what he would like to do in the service, he agreed to join the 101st Airborne Division. Because they were based at Fort Campbell Kentucky, near Hopkinsville, he felt he would be able to come home often. Unfortunately, the Army had different ideas for Art's future. After intensive schooling and additional paratrooper training, Art was sent to Vietnam. The war was winding down at the time and President Nixon was giving lip service to getting all the soldiers home. He felt this meant he would surely be stationed near his home. Art's company, however, was sent directly to the front lines at Saigon where they proceeded to assist with rescue efforts to bring the wounded out to the medic helicopters. He was flown behind enemy lines and he parachuted into the battlefields. He and his buddies feared for their lives every minute of every day. He managed to survive the skirmishes and was flown out of the war zone when the President finally called an end to the U. S. Military involvement in Southeast Asia. Many horror stories were embedded in his mind. Perhaps the two most recurring nightmares were about the facts that his two big brothers were actively protesting against a war in which he was daily risking his life; and the wasted lives he saw on the battlefield. However he staunchly refused to discuss the war or his experiences with anyone. Regardless of the circumstances, his life was changed forever and he continued to spend lonely times and sleepless nights alone. He was bedeviled with occasional flashbacks of the ghastly atrocities he had witnessed on the battlefield and what he felt was betrayal from his own siblings. Art was a good Christian and he prayed for his and his buddies' safety every day. He is sure the only reason he made it home was because God still had a plan for his life back in the states.

CHAPTER TWENTY-FIVE

The Tornado

    Jewel and Yvonne had continued to live in the house on Hanson St. in Jackson. Their church life continued as she maintained her active membership at First Christian Church. Missionary circles continued to meet at her home for luncheons and dinners. Jewel was a wonderful hostess and she always welcomed the opportunity to have the group come to her home. Life had not changed much for her except that she continued to purchase land in Leflore County. In 1992, she purchased the last piece of the original Harvey Treadwell farm. She was ecstatic at having fulfilled the promise to her dying father. She now owned all the parcels of land once owned by her father. The caretaker's house was rented to a family named Darnell. He was the son of one of Jewel's cousins. He was an excellent caretaker treating the property as if it were his own. He continued to look after the cabin and see that it was in reasonably good repair. The caretaker managed to handle Jewel's horses that were housed in a big barn across from the cabin. He also had other livestock;

everything from a ginny mule to a flock of peacocks. There were goats that they kept for milk; chickens for their eggs; calves that they butchered for their meat; and a few old bray horses that they kept for some unknown reason. The ginny was such an oddity that they kept it for conversation with the neighborhood children. Ben was a wonderful Christian and he served Jewel well. He would visit her and Yvonne when they came to the cabin and she delighted in talking with him about things of a spiritual nature. He was with her several years but finally he moved to Greenwood where he could be more involved in his church with his children's activities.

Finding a caretaker for the cabin and the tenant house became a real adventure. No one seemed to want to assume those duties. A couple from nearby Stantonville approached Jewel and asked to become her caretaker. She quickly accepted their offer and John and Margaret Wilson moved in the rental house. They have done an excellent job tending the property and have kept Yvonne and Jewel in summer produce since the day they moved in.

Jewel's first husband, Ward, had a sister named Mildred, who had been a little girl when she and Ward were first married. She was now grown and had married a man named Billingsley. They had a son named Benjamin. He was Jewel's only nephew on the Frederickson side of the family. Benjamin was an entrepreneur and an inventor. He developed a company called Fiberglow based in Leflore County in Carrollton. His company employed several of the area residents adding to the financial stability of an economically depressed area. His company manufactured fiberglass spas and hot tubs as well as related items. Benjamin seemed to understand what the hottest items were at the right time and how his financial involvement could make him a good return on his money. His investments paid a handsome return and Benjamin was "in the chips". Fiberglow became the largest manufacturer of spas and hot tubs in North America. Because of the necessity for air transportation to and from his company headquarters, Benjamin bought a piece of land near Coila. He developed a landing strip that would rival the San Francisco Airport in size for the exclusive use of the jets delivering and picking up executives as well as sales personnel to the plant. The airport is located off the beaten path in the middle of nowhere. There is no hangar or repair shop; just a landing strip. Because there was no access to refuel the jets, a large driveway and parking area was constructed on the roadside for easy access for the fuel tankers that came to tend to the jet aircraft. Travelers on the Coila road are always surprised at the amount of air traffic and the sheer size of the facility that was used primarily by Benjamin's company. Jackson, a larger community to the north had made arrangements to have the airport become the county facility and therefore open for public use. No doubt in the future, it will become a profitable and well-used entity for the entire community. After several years, Benjamin sold Fiberglow but maintained an investment company using part of the name

    Benjamin was not one to be idle for long and, with the blessings of the State; a marina at the Freeman area on the Florwood River was built. Time had eroded an area of the river making a "hollow" spot where the shores receded creating a wonderful pocket area in the river. In this pocket was a great location to build a marina for pleasure boats. Because of the location and popularity of the marina, several restaurants and shops located in the area. It was a wonderful investment and the development made Benjamin a wealthy man. It was a wonderful addition to that part of the River. The marina gave access to the many pleasure boats on the river a place to dock and dine. Freeman Landing has long been considered the "Catfish Capital of the World", a self-appointed title, no doubt. However it is a very popular vacation spot and Benjamin's marina was a great addition to the area. Continued success was not to smile on Benjamin. On a stormy night in 1993, fire broke out at the marina and burned the entire facility completely. While the fire consumed most of Benjamin's investment, it took with it the pleasure boats of many people. Since it is virtually impossible to adequately insure a marina, and to have enough liability insurance for such a disaster, he was left with virtually nothing of his initial investment. No cause for the fire was ever mentioned but the devastation of Benjamin's investment was obvious. There was never an investigation into the cause and most of the boat owners settled with insurance companies for their losses. Benjamin returned to his home in Leflore County where his wife and two daughters lived in a fine home in Carrollton.

Benjamin was a gentleman farmer, devoting his time to his investments. However as Jewel had begun to repurchase her father's farm Benjamin had asked to rent the land from her for a rental amount known only to them. Jewel envisioned the farm to be another profitable venture for the two of them so she agreed to rent most of the farm to Benjamin. Benjamin was an entrepreneur not a farmer and only made a limp attempt at farming. And, for some strange reason, felt he didn't need to pay his Aunt Jewel her just rent when it was due. He had become very wealthy with his inventions and Jewel's dream of the farm being farmed for profit was not in Benjamin's plan. However foolish he might have been, he failed to cultivate the farm or clear the land and most of it fell into an overgrown state. Just as Berthina had done, he made no effort to get someone else to do the farming for him. He let the land set idle. After so many years it was no longer tillable. There was a lot of timber on the farm, which could have been sold but he failed to pursue that avenue as well. For many years the farm simply laid fallow. It would be virtually impossible for anyone to eke out a living on the farm today. It might be sold to a developer for home sites, but Jewel Matthews had and continues to have an aversion to selling any of the land. And because there is little or no industry in that part of Leflore County, developers have not yet been interested in building home sites in the area.

In the middle 60's, a cousin of Jewel's approached her about opening a barbecue restaurant. J.T Darnell had never been successful at anything he had attempted before, but he convinced Jewel that he was an experienced barbecue chef. He only needed someone to help him get started in his new venture. He knew he could make a lot of money in such a business located on the highway where every one passed as they went to and from work each day. Jewel bought his story and selected a parcel of land across the highway from the cabin on the Carrollton road where J.T. could establish his eatery. She had a fine building built for him and outfitted it with all the equipment needed to open a good restaurant. Next to the business establishment, had been an old house. She had the house renovated and brought up to very good living standards for his family to live in and pursue their dream. She had the drive black-topped and a large sign erected stating the newest barbecue restaurant in Leflore County would soon be opening at this location. They had agreed on a 50/50-partnership agreement; that is 50% of the profits and free barbecue when she was in the area would be Jewel's share. Jewel loved barbecue so she thought the agreement a fair one. The restaurant opened and business was brisk, at first, however, at the end of the first year there were no "profits" for Jewel. By the end of the second year, J.T. was gone, having abandoned the building with all its equipment and had moved out of the house as well. He was last seen in the Jackson area delivering Pizzas. Jewel was left with her 50% and his.

Located on the farm, a short distance from Jewel's cabin is what is called the "Fossil Mound". At least that is what Jewel called it. It was a high mound of dirt that had layers and layers of sea fossils. Jewel remembered that her father had told her the story of how sea creatures had been deposited there during the Ice Age when the Gulf of Mexico reached to the shores of the Florwood River. The belief was that there was a cataclysmic eruption and the Florwood River reversed its course, causing it to flow north until it meets the Riley River. When the Polar Caps and glaciers began to melt the waters receded to the Continental borders, as we know them today. An archeologist and curator from the Jackson Museum examined the mounds and the fossils and verified that, indeed, they dated back to the Ice Age. In the 50's The National Geographic Magazine visited the area and studied the archeological finds. After a lot of study and testing of the soil and the fossils, they reported that the verification by the museum was correct. No mention of value was placed on the land or the products but no matter the price, Jewel would never sell an inch of that mound. Future generations may attempt to have it declared a valuable artifact site and forbid any further digging. Aside from all the historical and authentication of the Mounds, nearly everyone who had visited the cabin including Jewel's grandchildren have enjoyed their afternoons spent at the Fossil Mounds and have returned home with priceless artifacts rarely seen anywhere.

One summer in the early nineties, as Jewel and Yvonne were enjoying their visit to the cabin, a ferocious storm came up. The thunder and lightning were frightening. Yvonne was hysterical and frozen with fright. It was soon discovered the storm was a full-blown tornado. Jewel managed to get Yvonne to calm down and they took refuge on the inside wall in the center of the house, hoping this shelter would be adequate for the duration of the storm. The force of the tornado tore the roof off the house, demolished the front porch, and destroyed the barn across the road from the cabin. Jewel kept her horses in the barn with the idea that she would ride again one day. Needless to say, all of the horses were killed in the storm when the barn was demolished. The now defunct barbecue restaurant and house was completely blown away taking with it the sign that still bore the message of the future business. Jewel was left with a lovely blacktop driveway and nothing more to tell about what once had been her experience in the restaurant business.

Most of the community was in shock at the devastation they saw all around them. Houses had been blown away, livestock was scattered all along the fields, and trees had toppled on top of the highway. Electrical power was out in all the local communities and the highway from Greenwood to Carrollton was closed. Many of the power lines were down throughout the area and the danger of electrocution was everywhere. It was very dangerous for anyone to be out in the weather until some of the problems could be fixed. The torrential rains continued far into the night making repairs of the electrical problems even more difficult. If the tornado had traumatized most of the people around the community, Jewel was not one of them. She was never one to let the storms bother her. She had seen many storms in Leflore County and this was just one more, according to Jewel. In her effort to appear calm, she determined she could be of help. And anything she did was her method of keeping Yvonne calm. Yvonne was traumatized by this whole event and she could not see that anything could be repaired. She was sure they would all die in this storm. Jewel had no time to be afraid. She calmly built a fire in the cook stove and began brewing coffee and frying ham and eggs to feed the hungry workers. The linemen and electricians were on the job all night long. Jewel stayed right with them doing what she felt she should do, never mind that she was now seventy-eight years old.

Although the barn had blown away and the horses were all killed in the tornado, Jewel contacted her nephew Benjamin and instructed him to gather up the saddles, bridles, and other tack that he could salvage from the barn. She wanted him to store the paraphernalia in his barn indicating that she intended to get her another horse to ride in the near future. No one questioned Jewel as to the likelihood of her ever riding a horse again at her age. One just didn't do that.

CHAPTER TWENTY-SIX

Death of Percy

In the early part of 1992, Jewel received a call from the family of her only sibling, her half-brother, Percy. He had a heart attack and was not expected to live. He was living in Atlanta, Georgia. She boarded a plane to rush to his side. Jewel had stayed close to him for most of his life. Percy had been in the Army during the Korean War and had chosen to become a career soldier. He spent most of his lifetime away from Jackson or his other home in Leflore County. Because he had been in the Army for many years, he had lived in a number of cities. Jewel had visited him in some of them and would relate how his life was so different from hers. He had enjoyed his life in the military even though it was fraught with difficulties. His first wife had divorced him some years before he moved to Atlanta. From all accounts, Percy had a roving eye and had not been a faithful husband. His wife had reached a point when she had enough of sharing him with other women and sued him for a divorce. This action served to get his attention, and after some counseling, he chose to make another attempt at being married. He met a beautiful nurse named Mary Jane in Atlanta, and they were married in the 80's. She was a good mate for him and their life together was some of the best times of his life. Mary Jane was very close to Jewel and they had been friends for a long time. They had moved to Atlanta, with the intent of retiring to enjoy their senior years together. Fate had other ideas for Percy. His ideas of a peaceful retirement were thwarted when his heart attack proved fatal. He died before Jewel could reach him. She was greatly distressed that she had no opportunity to say a final goodbye to her only sibling, however, she felt sure he was a Christian so she took comfort in the fact that she would see him again in heaven. At the funeral, Jewel realized that everyone in her family was gone. She was now the standard bearer for the family long gone. For whatever reason, she knew God still had plans for her. She returned to Jackson and continued to care for Yvonne awaiting the next event that God had in store for her.

CHAPTER TWENTY-SEVEN

Mississippi D.O.T.

In the late nineties, the Department of Transportation decided to build a new highway through the middle of Jewel's farm. The old road that went from Greenwood to Carrollton had been a two-lane road and was well traveled. To build a four-lane highway they needed fifty feet off each side of the roadbed to widen the two-lane road. For many miles along the proposed highway route lay the land now owned by Jewel. If they chose to buy this land, it would mean that Jewel was selling part of the Treadwell farm. That thought alone caused Jewel to think through how she felt about selling any of her farmland. Selling was not her thing. They assured Jewel they would make her a new driveway to her cabin and landscape the ditch area to prevent the soil from washing away. They seemed willing to do about anything within reason to secure the good graces of this landowner. She pondered the idea, and again went to see her friend, Charlie Stanton. He was still a practicing attorney in Jackson, but now approaching eighty-five years of age. The State had offered

Jewel a large sum of money for the land however Jewel was not satisfied. She declared the land to be worth twice the price they were offering. The State considered her unreasonable and refused to meet her demands. The State Treasurer issued her a check for the original offer. Jewel was not the least bit enticed by the check and refused to cash it, placing it, instead, in a safety deposit box. This action threw the State into a quandary because they could not "close the transaction" even though the highway was nearly completed. They initiated negotiations with her and Mr. Stanton. Jewel refused to back down, and the State refused to increase the proposed price. Court action was the answer and the state proceeded to take the land by the process of Eminent Domain. (If land cannot be purchased by agreeable means, the state can declare the property necessary for the good of the public and seize it from the landowner). Jewel adamantly fought the state but did not win the Court battle. She finally agreed to put the check into an escrow account where it would, at least, bear interest until an agreement could be reached. As of this writing, the check still sits in the escrow account. It would be reasonable to assume that if it had been a Leflore County court case, Jewel Treadwell Matthews probably would have had her way; however, she didn't have much influence at the State level of government. For once in her lifetime, Jewel was stymied. She and Charlie Stanton had lost their battle, but not the war. She still awaits the outcome of the pending appeal. The question is; will she live long enough to see it settled or will her grandchildren consider her case folly and cash the check?

In 1998, the Mt. Pleasant Christian Church informed Jewel that the cemetery had no more burial lots. The community was a very old one and most of the older families had been buried in this cemetery. Their children and grandchildren were also interred in their family burial plots. Jewel wondered just what she should do about this dilemma. She had always felt she would be buried there. She had buried J.R. in the Memorial Park cemetery in Jackson however it had always bothered her. She wanted to be in Black Hawk, and she wanted him there with her. Now there was "no room in the inn". She pondered this problem for several months and finally decided the best thing to do was to donate some land to enlarge the Black Hawk cemetery. After all, this wasn't selling the land; it was giving back to the area that had given so much to her. She parceled off forty acres to be used as additional burial plots for the church cemetery, setting aside enough lots for J.R., Yvonne, and herself. She could now take comfort in the fact that when the time came, she could go home, at last.

CHAPTER TWENTY-EIGHT

The Grandchildren

Jewel's grandchildren were fully grown and gone from their mother's home. Belinda had little or no association with them. On many occasions, when they went to her home to visit, she refused to open the door. If they could get her to open the door, when she discovered who was at the door, she slammed the door mumbling something about this not being a good day. It was a real tragedy for the children to realize their mother was in a serious emotional state. And even more difficult to accept that she didn't want to see them. They still considered her their mother. Most of their parental guidance had come from their father, Kenneth Sr. and even that was sparse. He was not gifted with many parental skills and the children had basically grown up on their own. Ken Jr. had moved to San Francisco to life. He had not married and preferred a different lifestyle far away from the family's prying eyes. He returned to Jackson only on rare occasions to visit Jewel. Arthur was employed as a groundskeeper at the University Medical

Center. He had not married and lived most of the time with his granny. While his life was his own, Jewel still exacted her control over him, and from time to time he would move out to live on his own. On one occasion, he apparently felt smothered and he simply moved out unannounced on a Saturday morning. A visitor to Jewel's house that morning listened to Jewel rant on about his moving without any notice. When the visitor calmly mentioned that maybe he felt Jewel was too controlling of his activities, she belted out in her own inimitable way, " well, I am in control of his life, and he better get used to it." However every time Art saw the need to assist his granny he would move back in again. John, the third son, had married and had four girls including a set of twins. He, too, was a landscaper and was employed by Landover Baptist Church in Jackson. Landover is one of the largest churches in the south with a membership of about 20,000. Being a landscaper on staff was an important and well paying job. Johnny was very good at what he did and maintained a good living for his family. He rarely needed any funds from granny to support him. He seemed to be the mainstay of the family and continually attempted to handle the affairs at the farm for his grandmother. He had the love of the land that Jewel so admired. His attention to his heritage made him the "apple of her eye". He loved the old things that Jewel had kept that had once belonged to the family. Most of their possessions had burned in the fire, however Jewel had amassed a few photographs and memorabilia from other family members that she gladly passed on to Johnny. Jewel knew that he would take charge of all the details in the event of her passing. Jennifer, the only girl, was very much like her grandmother. She was headstrong and ambitious. Jewel often remarked that Jennifer was "what she always wanted to be". No one was sure what the interpretation of that comment was except to say that perhaps Jewel felt she would have liked an education. Jennifer was a small girl but had big ideas. She had become a physical therapist and was very good at her job. She had many clients that commented about her bedside manner. She was kind, considerate, and patient, even with her mother. From time to time, Belinda would allow Jennifer to give her a massage. She felt this would relax her and allow her to sleep better at night. Jennifer was delighted to spend even so little time with her mother. She felt Belinda needed help but she was helpless to meet her needs. Belinda preferred her own company to that of her children or anyone else. And that didn't appear to be changing.

CHAPTER TWENTY-NINE

The Gifts

Jewel continued to donate to various charities as well as the Mt. Pleasant Christian Church in Black Hawk. She generously supported the new library in Leflore County. On various occasions, she had paid a hospital bill for someone that needed surgery but had no insurance. These bills were sizeable, but she calmly wrote a check that amounted to thousands of dollars. One such incident involved a man who was facing open-heart surgery but had no insurance. The surgery was lifesaving but would have pushed his family into bankruptcy. They would have been left virtually penniless. The hospital in Jackson has a very good cardiac department. The surgery was scheduled for Monday morning. Jewel drove to the hospital the day of the surgery and inquired of the cost of such a procedure. Being told the cost would be in the thousands of dollars, she wrote out a check and left it with the hospital. The man's name was Lawrence McLean – it was never mentioned that he was the nephew of the man who had taken her father's life so long ago. No doubt this act was the ultimate in forgiveness. Doctors and nurses at the hospitals around Jackson and Leflore County had learned not to question any actions from the unpredictable Jewel Matthews.

When Christmas rolled around in 1995, Jewel decided to give each of her grandchildren a check for ten thousand dollars. She had given this gesture a lot of thought and felt this was the time to give them some money since each of them had a specific need, in her mind's eye. She wrote the check and handed them out as they visited her for the holidays. Art took his check and promptly gave it to the church where he was attending. Although he had no car and no personal possession, he calmly stated that he had a place to live; therefore he had no need for that much money. Jewel was astounded at his generosity, but it warmed her heart to realize he had learned a valuable lesson from his granny. His church meant more to him than money in the bank. John proudly told granny that he was able to get his family out of debt with her gift. Jennifer was able to get her education paid for and have some left over to buy a car enabling her to get back and forth to work without riding the bus. No word was ever heard from Ken Jr., as to whether he even received it. All of them handled the money in their own way without direction from Jewel.

Yvonne's health had continued to deteriorate. She was gaunt and frail. She could barely attend to her own personal hygiene needs on a daily basis. She continually needed direction from her mother. She was not able to help with the household chores. She did not have an exercise program, although her mother encouraged it. Jewel had been faithful to her own exercise regimen after the hip surgeries and she became frustrated with Yvonne when she refused to do anything to help herself. Jewel soon learned that Yvonne had a bit of her mother's constitution and rarely took orders from anyone including Jewel. She did very little except read and watch television. When the doctors diagnosed her with Parkinson's disease the news virtually ended all of her activities. She had a tremor in her arms, and that convinced Yvonne that she was unable to do anything for herself. Almost from that day forward, Yvonne retreated to her room and became a helpless invalid. Jewel made sure there was a nanny to care for her and Yvonne took to her room to enjoy the care she received. She no longer had to make any decisions or do anything she didn't want to do.

Jewel continued to entertain the visitors to First Christian Church with the help of a cook. Her knees and hips have long been the source of most of her aches and pains. But true to her philosophy, Jewel never complained. Her eye doctor informed her she had macular degeneration and her sight would eventually leave her completely. That was a cruel blow to Jewel since the one thing she had enjoyed since she was a small child would soon be out of her range of capabilities. She would no longer be able to read. She kept a radio by her bedside and listened intently to National Public Radio all day long, every day. When any program was on the radio that she wanted to hear, she would refuse to entertain visitors or take a phone call. She simply refused to be interrupted.

Jewel had a niece named Barbara Treadwell. She was the daughter of Harvey's youngest brother, John. John had been the storekeeper during the days when Harvey ran the gin. Barbara was his only daughter but when her mother died, he remarried immediately thereafter. Barbara was never consulted about what would happen to her mother's possessions and when she discovered his new wife had sold most of them at a "yard sale" she confronted her father about such crass actions. He defended his wife and said that most of the stuff was pure junk and he wanted to enjoy new furniture for the rest of his life. Needless to say, this caused a rift between her and her father. Barbara had worked for many years for a company called "Large and Tall Shop". She was based in New York with the parent company, but she was a "buyer" for them so she traveled the world. In 1998 the company was sold during a hostile takeover and the new management made many changes. Barbara had been faithful to the parent company for over 30 years however she was "downsized" right out of a job. She received a severance package but she was forced to return to Greenwood. After trying unsuccessfully to find other employment she soon realized the job market for someone her age was quite small. Barbara visited Aunt Jewel and discussed opening her own shop. She would feature large sizes and regular sizes plus a large line of gift items such as handbags, scarves, perfumes, and colognes. Barbara knew how to obtain this type of merchandise and she knew how to set up a shop. It would be a fashionable ladies boutique on the main street in Carrollton near the newspaper office. Jewel was delighted to see Barbara attempt to do something and she readily agreed to help her all she could. After only a short time the business closed. Barbara was savvy about the business, but what she didn't know was the demographics of the area. Most of the women in the small town of Carrollton either made their own clothing or purchased their needs at Wal-Mart. Almost no one ever came into the charming little boutique, much to Barbara's dismay. Jewel never mentioned the loss of her investment. She wanted to help and she did, the only way she could.

CHAPTER THIRTY

Jewel's Reflections

Age has taken its toll on Jewel. Upon reflection, she now has all the land she once promised her father she would "guard". However, most of the land had become a wasteland. She doesn't see it that way, since she feels pride in the ownership of the entire amount. She even begrudges the state the amount they took from the frontage of her property.

She has lost the respect of her oldest daughters because of her iron rule over her and her inability to identify the root problem. She mourns the break with her nephew over the rental of the farm. She would like to have a better relationship with Benjamin, but he is very busy with his own business ventures and rarely takes the time to see his aunt. She continues to allow him to rent the farm from her rather than withdraw the lease and let someone else take over the property. It is a shock to everyone that she has allowed this agreement to go unchallenged. Jewel would insist that anyone else pay the rent and pay it promptly. Why she is so generous with Benjamin is beyond imagination. And who will inherit the farm? Only Jewel knows the answer to that question. And what of the money that Jewel has amassed – she knows they don't make pockets in shrouds! Many questions go unanswered and it would take the wisdom of Solomon to solve them. One thing is for sure, regardless of what Jewel thinks, she knows she will not be immortal.

CHAPTER THIRTY-ONE

Final Musings

Jewel stood, steadied by her walker, at the bottom of the stairs. She looked up the darkened stairway longingly. Up those ominous stairs lay her baby daughter, now 69 years old and a helpless invalid. Nothing the doctors or nurses had been able to do made any change on the status of her health. Although Yvonne was not in pain, she could not sit erect but was curled in an almost fetal position. She had not seen her mother in more than three years; Jewel was unable to climb the stairs because of her hip problems and Yvonne could not go downstairs. She had been carried down on Christmas day a few years ago, but could only stay with the celebrating crowd for a short time. The excitement was too overwhelming. Although she loved every minute of the attention, she was simply unable to handle all the noise and commotion. When she was returned to her room, she commented that it probably would be her last trip. Medicine kept some of the trembling caused by the Parkinson's disease at bay, but nothing would cure the root cause. She spends her days watching television or movies on the VCR. She was aware of her condition and from time to time tears would fall softly on her pillow when she realizes she is terminally ill.

Jewel needed the replacement of her kneecap to be done again, but she refused to be put to sleep again. Jewel was not afraid of dying but she didn't choose to die under an anesthetic administered by a doctor, if she had a choice. And she considered her choice made. She spent most of her time just sitting by the window and listening to her radio, pondering the plight of her final days.

If only I could cradle her in my arms once more, Jewel thought, remembering the days when she and Yvonne had shared a life of ease. Her thoughts rambled through the many trips they had taken together. She reminisced about their summers at the farm. She could remember the days in school when Yvonne had such a difficult time with her studies. And now she seemed so far away. Jewel realizes that she is blessed by not being able to climb the stairway because she would have to see Yvonne in a fetal position, her limbs askew. Such a sight is not the memory she wants to carry with her for the rest of her days. Jewel also knows that she will see Yvonne again when they get to heaven where they both will have new bodies, free of pain and disease.

All the material things she has amassed; the house on Hanson St., the land she had regained over the last 50 years, restoring the name of the Harvey Treadwell Family in Leflore County, and all the money in the bank, seem to mean nothing now. She cannot buy Yvonne's health with any amount of money. She cannot buy Belinda's love; heaven knows she has tried. Her grandchildren are graciously awaiting her demise to reap the monetary reward they are sure their granny will leave them. She wonders if their love and affection is conditional. Even Kenneth Sr.'s attention is suspect. At a time when it seems that she should have it all, she realizes what an empty victory she has won. But she is content in the knowledge that she fulfilled a promise to her father made so many years ago. She has guarded the land.

She slowly closed her eyes and waited catching a glimpse of the life on the other side and knew it would not be long. Who will go first, she or Yvonne? What did it matter? Yvonne had been taken care of through a trust she set-aside for her. The grandchildren would handle the legal affairs. And what of Belinda? Would she ever reconcile before Jewel was gone? Jewel ponders that question, but quickly dismissed it from her mind. She can still remember the threat Belinda had made about not being at Jewel's funeral. She only knows that she cannot live with regrets so she pushes the Belinda questions out of her mind. She has very few friends left. She had been to the funeral for most of the people she had known for so many years. They are all gone now. In spite of her knee and hip problem, Jewel is in reasonably good health. She has been a widow for more than 40 years and still yearns for the times she spent with J.R. and their life together. She can scarcely think about him without it bringing tears to her near sightless eyes. She will never forget him. He was the best thing that ever happened to her and she knew it from the start.

Jewel cries softly to herself and shuffles back across the room to her chair. It is only a matter of time, she says. Only heaven awaits.

EPILOGUE

Belinda slipped quietly into the back of the chapel. She was bereft. So much time lost, she thought. Oh, why did I let it go by! The tears flowed freely from her eyes and dropped unceremoniously on her simple black dress. Jennifer tried to console her mother but seemed helpless to reach her. Belinda could still remember the day she fled from the house on Hanson St., vowing never to return. Now she could feel nothing but regret. All she ever wanted from her mother was her love. Jewel always seemed unable to give that emotion to her first born. If Belinda was helpless to accept her authoritative nature as a sign of affection, Jewel was equally unable to change her methods. Jewel never realized that what Belinda wanted most was her mother's acceptance for what she was; a person with severe depression. Now it was too late. Belinda slowly rose to leave before anyone noticed. She left the church in a depressed state of mind and returned to the solitude of her home on Veolla St. With the shades drawn she, once more, retreated into the world of Belinda.

The hearse from the Frederickson funeral home slowly wound its way into the Black Hawk Cemetery's newest plot of ground.

There on a mound were two fresh graves. One was open and the other recently closed. The headstone proudly stated the Jewel of Leflore County, a name given to her by the Doctor on the day she was born, and the two names engraved were J.R. MATTHEWS and JEWEL TREADWELL MATTHEWS. Jewel was home in Leflore County, at last.

THE END

ABOUT THE AUTHOR

Alyce Godbey was born and reared in Southwest Indiana, the youngest of six children. She relates in many personal ways to her "rags to riches: character, Jewel, in her journey through Depression Era to the present. The author brings her own experiences to the novel of career ambitions, travel, family trials and traumas, and a "never-give-up" world-view often reflected in her characters.

Although she is new to the fiction writing world, she has years of writing experience for journals and magazines.

The author currently lives in Southwest Indiana with her husband. Together they run a Bed and Breakfast in a small town.

Printed in the United States
64644LVS00003B/252